SWALLOWING FIRE

STARCROSSED DRAGONS BOOK 3

ERIN BEDFORD

J. A. CIPRIANO

WANT TO GET FREE STUFF?

<u>Sign up here.</u> If you do, I'll send you some free short stories.

Visit Erin on Facebook or on the web at ErinBedford.com.

ALSO BY ERIN BEDFORD

<u>The Underground</u>

Chasing Rabbits

Chasing Cats

Chasing Princes

Chasing Shadows

Chasing Hearts

<u>Fairy Tale Bad Boys</u>

Hunter

Pirate

Thief

Mirror

Stepbrother

The Celestial War Chronicles

Song of Blood and Fire

Visions of War and Water

The Mary Wiles Chronicles

Marked By Hell

Bound By Hell

Deceived By Hell

Tempted By Hell

The Crimson Fold

Until Midnight

Vampire CEO

Granting Her Wish

ALSO BY J.A. CIPRIANO

<u>Starcrossed Dragons</u>

Riding Lightning

Grinding Frost

Swallowing Fire

Pounding Earth

<u>The Goddess Harem</u>

The Tiger's Offer

The Wolf's Hunt

The Dragon's War

<u>Justice Squad</u>

Miracle's Touch

<u>Her Angels</u>

Heaven's Embrace

Heaven's A Beach

Heaven's Most Wanted

The Shaman Queen's Harem

Ghosts and Grudges

1

———

I used to love snow, especially on Earth. The first few flakes seemed like a magical experience every winter. I anticipated the first snowfall every year, longing to see that white powder cover the trees and the ground.

Not so much now.

If I never saw snow again, I would die a happy woman.

In Waesigar, the snow was not magical. It was just wet. And cold. It crawled into every crevice of your clothing until you were soaked through and your skin went numb.

Flying through it was worse because the small flakes of snow which seemed so harmless on the ground were now flying daggers intent on ripping the skin from my face.

I couldn't wait to get into something dry and warm and a hot bath? That seemed like a dream come true for my aching bones.

"Fuck it's cold," I cried, hugging myself as my new wings beat ceaselessly at the stupid frozen air. They ached like a son of a bitch because I still wasn't used to them. Sure, being able to fly was awesome, but flying in a blizzard for days after getting said wings? Not so much.

"Well, it is the frozen north," Jack said, smiling at me and trying to calm me with his stupid smile. "And we'll be there soon."

"You said that a week ago and yet here we are, still frozen." I glared at him as Firestar flew over to me from where he'd been at the front of the group, but even his superheated presence didn't help. He was but a candle to the wrath of winter.

"Are you doing all right back there?" Firestar asked, real concern in his voice. Jack and Raiden flanked me. On the surface, it seemed like we were making good time, but if I was being honest with myself, I knew I was holding us back and making us have to stay out longer in the cold.

"I'm fine," I yelled back over the whipping wind, but it came out more like a breathless squeak.

Raiden and Jack signaled to each other, something they often did, and never stopped to explain to me what they meant.

"Let's take a break," Jack commanded, pointing down to the ground.

My pride wanted me to argue, to reiterate that I was fine, but if I flew anymore, I would crash down on the snow-covered ground below. Then there would be no point in being able to fly in the first place.

We descended from the sky, but sadly there was no pretty clearing to make camp in. Nor trees for wood to build a fire. There was only miles and miles of snow-covered hills. I had been lucky to buy some clothing from the village we had passed on the way, or I really would have frozen to death by this point.

As we landed on the ground, my boots sunk into the foot-deep snow, and I rubbed my hands together to try to get some feeling back into them.

Glancing over at Jack, I noticed he wasn't pink-cheeked and shivering like the rest of us. "Cold really doesn't bother you, does it?"

Jack shrugged an elegant shoulder, still only clad

in one of his expensive suits. "Not particularly. Low temperatures don't bother ice dragons much."

I wrapped my arms around myself, shivering through my thick jacket. I let my wings disappear, no longer having the energy to keep them out. Raiden brought me one of the blankets we kept rolled up in our packs and wrapped it around my shoulders. I took it with a grateful smile and watched as Firestar made our camp.

Out of all my dragons, Firestar was the one I worried the most about in the cold weather. Hot by nature, I'd thought he would have it worse than me, but he barely had a pink hue to his cheeks and only wore a leather jacket over his shirt and pants. Maybe his inner flame was keeping him warm?

He and Raiden cleared out some of the snow revealing the frozen ground beneath it. It looked like they were going to make a fire, but even if they did, there were no trees to burn.

"I really hope your brothers thought of everything or this is going to be the world's shortest pit stop," Firestar said, pulling out a dark purple bag with an intricate design of magic symbols that Raiden's brothers had given us before we'd fled their lands.

"Me too," Raiden replied, rubbing his hands

together as Firestar began to rummage around in the bottomless bag. "It'd be silly not to pack fire-wood though since it can hold a nearly infinite amount of stuff." He snorted. "That's why they cost more than most kingdoms."

"Guess wishes are horses." Firestar reached into the bag and withdrew a bundle of wood before holding it out triumphantly. "Your brothers aren't as dumb as I'd thought. Thank god."

Raiden snorted before taking the wood from Firestar. "Here let me set it up. I've got a special trick that makes it easy to light no matter the weather." He nodded to himself as he began to arrange the wood on the driest spot he could find, which wasn't much since the snow had made everything damp. He carefully arranged the differing branches into a teepee where the inner layer was made from the thinnest, easiest to burn twigs before moving to heavier and heavier sticks.

"There." He nodded triumphantly to himself when he was done. "Now let me just get the flint and we'll—"

A ball of white-hot flame burst from Firestar's outstretched hand, whipping right by Raiden and smacking into the fire with a whoosh.

"Hey!" Raiden shouted jumping up from the

ground and beating at his clothing where the fire had singed him. "Watch where you're aiming that thing."

Firestar grinned, not at all sorry. "Then learn to move."

He plopped the bag down on the ground and held his arm out to me. I didn't think twice about curling into his warm embrace, his internal heat was far greater than my own.

Leaning my head against Firestar's chest, I watched the flames burn and tried to be grateful that no one had chased us so far.

Instead, I did my best to let the fire melt all my troubles and over analyzing away. I wished I could be as carefree as the flames. They jumped and swirled almost like they were dancing. It was so mesmerizing I didn't realize I had fallen asleep until Firestar shifted to wake me.

"Come, Maya," he murmured into my ear and gave me a little nudge. "We must keep moving. It's not far now."

"Mmm," I mumbled, snuggling close to his warmth. "Just five more minutes."

"No." Firestar stood, causing me to face plant into the cold ground.

Mother fucker. Mouth full of wet ground, I

sputtered as I sat up. Letting out a growl, I glowered up at the fire dragon. "What was that for?"

Smirking, Firestar began to pack up the camp. "I know you well enough to know five more minutes means five more hours."

I couldn't really argue with that. I wasn't a morning person. Hell, I wasn't even a day person. If there was one thing I valued more than anything in this world, it was my sleep. I doubted that would change when I finally became pregnant. In fact, it would probably be worse, and I for one was looking forward to squirreling away my pregnant self for the winter and sinking into blissful slumber.

"Still! You didn't have to drop me," I snapped as I climbed to my feet. "I'd have gotten up … eventually."

"Yes, well, I'd like to get to Jack's home before nightfall, and we've already waited long enough." Firestar nodded toward the sun only a few feet above the horizon. We wouldn't make it by nightfall if I flew, I knew that better than any of them.

"How are your wings?" Jack asked, rubbing his hand on my back.

I tried to put on a strong face but failed. Sighing, I rubbed the back of my shoulders myself, trying to help Jack ease the aches. "Sore, tired. I'm not used to flying so much. Or at all."

"It'll get better," Jack reassured me, his hand still caressing my back. "You have just begun to learn. You can't push yourself so hard. No matter what anyone says." He shot an icy glare at Firestar who ignored him.

"He's right, Maya," Raiden said after he finished putting out the fire. The cold winds that replaced it made me miss it already. "Even as children, most of us could only fly for short periods at a time in the beginning. You're already doing far more than you should."

"I know," I sighed and flipped my braided hair over my shoulder. "I was just so happy to not be a burden anymore. I couldn't bear to ask you to stop or carry me."

"Maya." Firestar snapped his hard gaze on me. "Do you really think we'd stick around for all this crap if we thought you were a burden?"

"Well, no." I frowned and shuffled my feet.

"Then don't bring it up again. We're here for you. If you need something, tell us. If you're tired, say so. And if you want one of us to carry you, just ask." Firestar stopped in front of me and smacked me on the backside, making me yelp.

"Or I'll throw you over my lap and tan your hide red."

Raiden smiled broadly at his words, and I knew the dragon was all too eager to have the threat come to life.

"Fine, fine," I finally conceded and turned to Jack. "Would you mind carrying me the rest of the way?"

"It'd be my honor," Jack half bowed, making me giggle as he stood and pulled me into his arms.

The ride this time wasn't as bad. The air was still cold, and Jack's frosty body temperature didn't really help, but at least I wasn't tired. I probably should have asked Firestar to carry me since I wouldn't have been so cold, but my backside still stung after his little stunt, and I didn't want to give him the opportunity for more teasing.

Eventually, when the sun had just set, we landed on a large hill just outside of a village. The wind had died down, but the snow had begun to fall. Even back on Earth, I'd never seen so much snow in one place, and I'd lived on the upper east coast.

Jack's home reminded me of those little elf towns they made back on Earth during their winter celebrations. The homes looked to be wooden huts with chimneys blowing gray smoke into the air, twirling above the rooftops in wispy curls, almost making a design. The palace itself wasn't a stone and mortar type of home like the rest of ours, but an even larger wooden hut with metal reinforcements holding it together. I suddenly wondered where the humans had gotten such an idea from and if it had been us or them who had stolen it.

"Jack," I gasped, my mouth open as I stared at the sight. "It's wonderful."

"Yes, it is," he agreed with that soft smile that was usually reserved for me alone.

"So, if you are the nephew of Lord Fafnir," Raiden asked and pointed down into the village, "where do you live? Certainly not the palace?"

", I do," Jack answered, and a sadness covered his face. "My parents passed away not long ago, and since there is not a lot of wood to spare, we tend to live with relatives even when we have a family of our own." He gave Raiden a smug look. "So, I do live in the palace."

"Oh," was all Raiden said in response. He wasn't the only one who didn't know how to respond to Jack's reveal of his heritage. I wished I'd learned about it long before now.

I stood and placed my hand on Jack's arm, knowing it was the only form of comfort I could provide that he would accept for something like this. He glanced down at me, his pale eyes filled with emotion, and it almost had me in tears.

"Jack, I-" I started to say but was cut off when something hit my nose. It was an awful scent, a mixture of burning meat and rotten eggs that made me gag. I barely spun around fast enough before my body rejected the contents of my stomach.

I threw up until there was nothing, but dry heaves left. A hand rubbed my back as another held my hair away from my face. My chest heaved as I glanced to see Jack and Raiden helping me. Firestar stood a bit apart from us, looking a bit green himself.

I was lucky we hadn't eaten much on the way here, or I'd been throwing up even more. Why the sudden smell had caused such a reaction was beyond me. I usually had a strong stomach, so much so that Ryan on Earth and I used to have eating contests to see who would eat the most disgusting concoctions.

Well, except when I was on my period. Usually, during those times, I just wanted to roll in piles of chocolate and watch sappy movies. Now, though, even the thought of chocolate made my stomach jump, and I braced myself for more dry heaving.

When none came, my mind reminded me that my period should have hit on the way to Jack's home. The fact that it hadn't made my stomach roll. Sweat dripped down my back as a horrible realization came to mind.

"Guys," I swallowed thickly and licked my dry lips as all three of them leaned in to listen. "I think - this time - I might actually be pregnant."

Thud.

I jerked up to my feet, instantly regretting it because of the wave of dizziness that came with it. I grasped blindly for a handhold and found Jack's arm. When the world stopped spinning, I searched the area for what had caused the sound. What I found was Firestar passed out cold in the snow.

Well, that was just great.

2

The magnitude of what I had just realized didn't help my swirling insides. Nor Firestar's collapse. Who would have guessed that out of all my men, he'd be the one to freak out?

Well, he'd have to wait. I didn't have time to baby him since I still hadn't wrapped my head around the possibility of being pregnant. If I was even pregnant.

Stomach still in turmoil, I let Jack lead me to a dry patch to sit. Raiden knelt by Firestar, an all too amused smirk on his face.

"Just leave him for now." I sighed and rubbed a hand over my face. A hand full of snow came into my line of sight. With a curious frown, I followed the hand up to Jack's concerned face.

"For your mouth," he explained, nodding for me to take it.

"Don't we have anything else?" I glanced toward our bottomless bag.

Jack gave me an exasperated look. "Yes, but why waste resources when there is plenty of snow to go around."

Still frowning, I took the freezing ball of snow from Jack and brought it to my mouth. The snow liquefied in my mouth instantly cooling the heat my sickness had left behind. I turned and spat out the warmed snow and then took another bite. The taste wasn't as bad now but still there. I'd need something more substantial to get rid of the acrid taste altogether.

"Better?" Jack asked, placing a hand on my arm.

I nodded slowly, still aware of my knotting stomach.

"Should I try to wake him?" Raiden asked with a quirked brow.

Shrugging, I dropped the rest of the snow in my hand to the ground, rubbing my cold hand on my pants. "Unless one of you wants to carry him the rest of the way?"

Jack snorted, and Raiden smiled broadly. "Wake up time it is."

Drawing a hand back, Raiden prepared to smack Firestar awake. Normally, I would be against violence between the guys – training aside – but Firestar's reaction kind of bugged me. If he couldn't even handle the news that I might be pregnant what would happen when I actually was?

Raiden's hand came down and was just inches from Firestar's face before Firestar caught his wrist. Eyes flashing red, Firestar sat up and shoved Raiden away.

"Don't even think about it," Firestar growled at him before his eyes landed on me. They softened considerably, and if I wasn't mistaken, had a bit of worry in them. Firestar was by my side faster than I could blink, holding my hand and looking me over.

"Are you, all right?"

"Just peachy," I grumbled, staring down at our joined hands. While mine were still a bit numb from the snow, his were molten hot, and the warmth of his touch made me feel a lot better.

Firestar cupped my face in his hands, drawing

my eyes to his. "Do you think you're really…" His eyes darted down to my stomach, and I groaned.

"I don't know. Maybe. Or it could be something I ate." The mixture of disappointment and relief on his face didn't go unnoticed. So, I quickly added, "But we have been humping like bunnies for the last few months so if I weren't by now…" I trailed off, lifting one shoulder.

Thankfully, before Firestar could prod me more, Jack stood and announced, "We can find out for sure at the compound. Right now, all we are doing is wasting time. Maya?" His pale eyes landed on me in question. "Are you all right to keep going? It's not much further."

Nodding, I moved to stand, but Firestar beat me to it, hauling me to my feet without a word. I glared at him, but he didn't seem to notice. This was going to be annoying.

After gathering up our supplies, we started back toward Jack's home. He'd been right when he'd said it wasn't much further. We only walked for about twenty minutes before a settlement came into view. Flying was out of the question, I didn't trust my stomach to behave. What a first impression that would be!

Jack's home was nothing like the others. Raiden,

Firestar, and I were all from ruling families. We were used to seeing large palaces with an even bigger city sprawled beneath it. That wasn't what was before us now.

There was a town all right, but I bet I could walk from one end of it to the other in a matter of minutes.

The houses in the town were more like huts and were made of wood and straw. Still, they did have stone mixed into the foundations, but it was nothing like what I'd seen in the other kingdoms. Hell, even the so-called palace wasn't much of a palace at all and was made of the same material as the rest of the houses. Sure, it was larger, but it was nothing like the massive monstrosities the other Lords had.

"It's so…" I drew out as we approached the compound gates, frowning when no guard stopped to question us. "Quaint."

"Yes, it is." Jack seemed proud of it. Having grown up in a large city myself, I couldn't really bash what he considered home. In a way, it made sense. Jack, despite his fancy suits, never seemed the kind to care about how badass or rich he looked. He just was. His home fit him perfectly.

As we walked through the town, many of the residents looked up from their tasks to watch us.

Several of them even bowed in respect to Jack; others shouted out his name with a wave of their hand.

To my surprise, Jack waved back. A genuine smile on his face.

"You must be happy to be home," I commented, taking a few steps closer to him so that my arm bumped his.

Jack surprised me once more by grasping my hand in his as he smiled softly down at me. "It is nice to be back, but it wouldn't be home unless you were here."

I fought back a blush and stared down at my feet. Jack sure knew how to make a girl feel wanted. I glanced back at Raiden and Firestar who had started to trail us and couldn't help but laugh.

While the villagers had been happy to see Jack, they were curious about my other two companions. The villagers stared at them as they followed closely, the eyes on them no doubt making them uncomfortable. Or at least Firestar. Raiden seemed to gobble up the attention, waving and winking at the spectators.

"Attention whore." I scoffed loud enough to be heard.

"I heard that," Raiden called to me, not deterred from basking in the attention.

"You were meant to," I countered back and giggled.

Firestar grunted in response to our joking and hurried his pace until he was on my other side. I took his hand in mine as well, not bothered by the surprised looks I received from the villagers.

While it wasn't unheard of for a dragon to have more than one mate, most of them didn't flaunt it in public. I wasn't going to be like that. If I was going to be in a relationship with all three of them, I was going to let everyone know. I wanted them to know I wasn't ashamed of them. Plus, it didn't hurt to make sure all those leering females knew who belonged to who.

"Be nice," Jack muttered in my ear, startling me.

"What?"

"You look about a second away from tearing those women's faces off," Firestar whispered and squeezed my hand tightly in warning though there was amusement on his face.

"I am not."

"Your face does not lie," Jack informed me before stopping to cup my face in his hands. He brushed his lips across mine in a quick kiss. "Jealousy does not become you, though flattering."

My face heated. I wasn't jealous. Okay, maybe a little bit. But I'd gone through hell and back to secure my little squad. I wasn't about to lose them to some horny village girls.

We passed through the market area, which wasn't much more than a few wooden stalls. Some had wares till displayed, clay pots, bags of herbs, but most seemed ready to go home for the day. Not surprising since the sky had darkened considerably since we arrived.

As we made our way past the center of the market, warmth touched me. A pit sat in the middle with a small fire going giving the air a burning wood smell. Better than the mixture of manure and piss some of the cities had.

The smells aside, we were close to the main house now, and still, no one came out to greet us as the other regions had. I worried we might actually have to knock on the door which would be embarrassing in itself. Who knocks on their own home?

Then just as we reached the large double doors with intricate carvings of dragons and ice decorating the wood, they swung open. Several guards came out, each dressed in similar dark brown leather pants and long-sleeved shirts, their pale hair braided down their backs. It was then I noticed that like the guards most of the villagers had also been wearing clothing that one would see in summer and not deep in the snowy mountains.

"Do all ice dragons have an immunity to the cold?" I asked Jack but didn't get an answer as more people poured out of the house.

A man as tall as Jack with long white hair and eyes as white as snow smiled at us. Like Jack, he had a taste for expensive suits, and I knew without a doubt this had to be Lord Fafnir.

"My dear nephew," Lord Fafnir announced, his hands behind his back. Unlike Raiden's father, Lord Shen, he didn't move to embrace Jack or any of the rest of us. I couldn't say I was unhappy about it. I'd had far too many hugs from strangers as it was.

"Uncle." Jack inclined his head and then did the same to a man who was a younger replica of Lord Fafnir, and a woman I could only assume was his aunt. "I am glad to see you once more."

"And we you," Lord Fafnir replied before turning his attention to me. "This must be the lovely Maya. I am overjoyed to see you, my dear, the rumors of your beauty don't do you justice."

"Thank you." I flushed at his compliment. I

knew where Jack got his sweet talking from now.

As Lord Fafnir's eyes went from me to Firestar and Raiden, confusion flittered across his face briefly before vanishing under an icy mask. "And who are your other friends? We were only expecting the two of you."

Jack tensed beside me, but I didn't give him the chance to make up some kind of story. Instead, I stepped out from between them and said, "These are my other mates, my Lord. This is Firestar, first son of Lord Amun, and this is Raiden, third son of Lord Shen."

"Other mates?" The younger replica of Lord Fafnir gaped, and my gaze snapped to him.

"Yes," I answered my eyes narrowed, daring him to challenge my words. I was tired of people judging my decision.

"Tyrell, where are your manners?" Lord Fafnir waved a hand at the man and then turned back to me. "Please forgive my son. He's just surprised is all. When I saw you coming, I had assumed you had chosen my nephew for your mate, but I can see now that I was mistaken."

"Oh." I pressed my lips into a thin, annoyed line. I wasn't sure what to say to that even if I believed it.

Raiden didn't have that problem though. "Lord Fafnir let me be the first to say you have a lovely town. I wish my father put less effort into making us look intimidating and more into making it a home."

The tension eased out of Lord Fafnir as he turned to the lightning dragon and offered him a small smile before gesturing to the woman on his right. "That is my lovely wife, Ingrid's doing. She wouldn't allow such resources to be wasted when we have sparse few as it is."

Lady Ingrid nodded her head slightly, her pale hair tied up in an intricate knot on her head. Unlike the men, she wore a deep purple form-fitting leather dress that split in the front showing her brown leather encased legs. Couldn't fault them for functionality even in the royal house.

"Well, she has done a lovely job." Raiden smiled at the older woman causing her to blush. I rolled my eyes at his flirting. I swear, he could flirt with a rock.

"Now that we have all the pleasantries out of the way, how about we find you some rooms." Lord Fafnir swept a hand to the side gesturing for us to enter the house in front of him.

"Thank you, uncle." Jack led the way as we entered the main house. I stayed close to his side as my eyes took in his home. Lord Fafnir hadn't been kidding when he said Lady Ingrid didn't allow for wastefulness. While Lord Amun's palace had looked ransacked without any decorations of any kind, Lord Fafnir's held a more simplistic hue. No elaborate tables or pointless tapestries filled the halls. Instead, there was a strange fur theme. Fur rugs and coverings on the windows, it was almost as if we were inside of a big bear.

"The fur keeps the cold out," Jack murmured into my ear as if reading my mind or in this case my confused face.

"But you don't feel the cold," I reminded him, feeling a bit silly that I had to say it.

"Yes, but it's not about me. It's about the comfort of our guests." He gave me a knowing look which made my mouth form an o. More and more Lord Fafnir was proving to be a better lord than the rest. No money wasted so he could flaunt his position, and he had even thought of the other elemental dragon's comfort even if it did nothing for his own.

My father could learn a thing or two.

Lord Fafnir lead us down the hallway, pointing out different areas of the house before stopping at a hallway lined with doors. Frowning, he stood next to one of the doors and if I could have guessed he seemed a bit embarrassed.

"As I said before we had only been expecting Jack and Maya, so we only had two rooms prepared." His eyes glanced at me as he continued. "I didn't want to hope you were sharing a room already, so I had two prepared, but it will take a little time to get another two rooms ready."

"Not a problem." Firestar stepped forward, his large form filling much of the space, making the hallway feel smaller. "We can share until you are ready. It is our fault for not sending word ahead."

Lord Fafnir had a good poker face that was for sure. He didn't show an inch of nervousness in Firestar's presence. I couldn't say the same for his son who had visibly blanched at Firestar's menacing form.

"Very well," Lord Fafnir confirmed with a nod. "I will have the servants prepare more rooms at once but feel free to rest before dinner."

Firestar took my hand and opened the door to the first room. I glanced back to see Raiden shaking his head as he headed for the room across the hall. At least one of us knew not to cause drama.

I stopped at the door as I waited to see what Jack would do. He didn't move to follow Raiden or us into the room, and he had his guarded face on. That couldn't be good.

"Jack?" I raised a brow.

Offering me a small smile, Jack stepped toward me. "I will be along shortly. I want to discuss our current issue with my uncle in a non-hostile environment." His eyes went behind me to where Firestar stood in the room.

Chewing on my lower lip, I nodded. "Sure, I get it. Please be careful though."

"Of course." Jack cupped the side of my face, and I leaned into his touch. "Get some rest, and I will ask about getting you checked out with the medics."

Mentioning the medics reminded me of what had happened just before we came. Like I could forget. My stomach rolled just thinking about it, and I swallowed thickly.

"Okay. Sure." I didn't dare nod, fearing I'd lose what little else was in my stomach all over Lord Fafnir.

"Take care of her," Jack ordered Firestar over my shoulder earning him a grunt in response. He smiled once more at me before I closed the door and raced to the bathroom.

3

Warm. I was too warm. Rolling over, I moved away from the impossibly strong heat and sat up.

Firestar lay beside me, out cold. After I'd dry heaved into the toilet, Firestar had laid down with me, rubbing my stomach in small circles until I fell asleep. I supposed he was trying to make up for his passing out earlier.

Sighing, I slowly tossed the covers off and slid from the bed. Hands shot out around my waist pulling me back into the bed with an "Oof!"

"Where do you think you are going?" Firestar growled as he nuzzled my neck, his lower half grinding into my backside. Someone was thrilled to see me.

"To find something to eat," I told him, sinking into his embrace for a moment before adding, "Then I have to see if Jack made my appointment with the medic."

Firestar went quiet and shifted behind me before he asked, "Where are we?"

Letting out a slight chuckle, I twisted a bit to see his face. Confusion filled his eyes as they scanned the canopy above us. "You've forgotten already?"

His mahogany eyes scanned the room around us. It was nicer than I expected from Lord Fafnir's explanation of wasting resources. The fur theme from the rest of the house followed into here as well. Even the canopy above our heads was made of fur. The dresser had antlers for handles and legs, as did the nightstand. I felt like I was living in a hunting lodge or something.

Seemingly remembering our location, Firestar wrapped his arms around me once more, his hand going to my stomach and I knew what he would ask next.

"So, do you think you're pregnant? More importantly, do you want to be?"

I shrugged a shoulder. "I don't know. This was kind of the whole point of this thing, right? Besides, if I don't get pregnant than Ned has a better chance at the throne, and we so don't want that."

"Then we should find out for sure."

I rolled my eyes. "I would if you got your big butt off of me."

"Big butt, huh?" he growled into my ear, his hands sliding up from my stomach to my hips. "Are you sure it wasn't something else too large for you?"

I giggled at his antics but shook my head. Talking of Firestar's size caused me to think of Jack's size and how Firestar would react to it. Raiden didn't seem to have a problem with confidence, he had it in abundance. Firestar, on the other hand, would have a cow if he found out, which was why I wouldn't be telling him anytime soon.

"Pretty sure it wasn't."

Firestar didn't seem to like my answer, a low rumble coming from his chest. The hands on my hips dipped lower, slipping between my thighs and into my pants before I knew it. I wiggled my bottom against his front and arched against him as his fingers stroked me, causing a dull ache to develop.

"Tell me," Firestar demanded, his fingers fast at work bringing me higher and higher.

I gasped and moaned, "Tell you what?"

"Tell me you want it." He ground against my butt, demonstrating what exactly he wanted me to say.

"I want it," I croaked as Firestar's fingers slid inside of me. I thrust myself into his grasp, seeking to feel him deeper. Firestar seemed more than ready to give it to me as he repeatedly plunged his fingers into me.

Just as I was about to reach my release, his hand froze. I cried out in frustration and smacked his side with my hand. "What the hell?"

"The baby can't feel me doing this, can he?"

The question was so absurd, I burst out laughing. When Firestar tensed behind me, I realized he was serious and choked back my amusement. "I'm sorry, I don't mean to laugh. I just ..." I shook my head and changed my tone. "No, Firestar. If I am in fact pregnant, the baby couldn't feel it. I'm not even showing yet. It can't be much more than a bundle of cells."

"Well, if you are sure ..." Firestar trailed off before jerking my pants down my legs. I ached in response, eager to continue where we left off.

Grasping my leg in his hands, he lifted it so that it was over his as he shifted his hips before pressing into me. I groaned as he filled me to the brim. I reached back behind me, my hand seeking something to hold on to. My fingers laced into his hair, clutching at his silky locks.

Hot and hard, Firestar angled his hips until he hit the spot inside of me that made me let out a choking gasp. Hitting that same spot in quick succession, it wasn't long until I had hit my release, my hands pulling at his hair. Firestar let go of my hips and cupped my breast in his hands, using it to drive me harder into his length.

Firestar tensed against me and let out a throaty groan before burying his sweat covered forehead against my neck. I stroked his head as I caught my own breath, my heart racing in my chest.

"What time did you say you were supposed to go see the medic?" he asked, moving away from me and getting out of the bed.

I had no shame as I watched him walk across the room to dig through his bag where the guys had dumped it. God, I could bite that ass.

As if he could read my mind, Firestar glanced back over his shoulder with a knowing grin.

Shaking my head at him, I sat up on the bed. "I don't know. I was just going to head that way and see if they'd see me."

"I'm going with you," Firestar stated as he pulled on clean clothes from his bag.

"I didn't expect anything less." I got out of bed, tugging my pants back up around my waist. "I'm sure Raiden and Jack will want to be there too."

Firestar frowned. The look on his face made me wonder if he had forgotten that the child might not be his. I hoped I wasn't looking at a future problem.

"Hey." I came up next to him, placing my hands on his shoulders. "We still have to find out if I'm pregnant. We can worry about whose it is when the time comes."

"And what if it's not mine?" His expression was far more tortured than I expected it to be. Firestar had always been an optimist.

"Then we'll deal with it then." I squeezed his arms with a reassuring smile, but he didn't return it.

"That's what you keep saying, but what does that mean?" He shrugged my hands off, moving around me to sit on the edge of the bed. He swapped out the shirt he had passed out in for another one of almost the exact same tan shade. "How exactly are you going to handle it?"

I opened my mouth to answer but came up empty. Firestar was right. When the time came, I didn't know what we would do. Hell, unless there was some kind of distinguishing features, I didn't even know how we would know whose it was.

Well, we could go back to the human world. I knew they had medical tests that could tell us who the father was, but it wouldn't solve the problem of what to do with the results. Had I been stupid to think that we would stay together forever? That having a child wouldn't change anything? The very idea of losing one of them made it hard to breathe, to think, to live.

"Would you leave?" I croaked, trying to hold back the tears that threatened to spill. "If the child isn't yours, would you leave me?"

When Firestar met my eyes, his intense expression softened. Standing from the bed, he crossed the room and scooped me up into his arms. Pressing his forehead to mine, he murmured, "Of course not. I made the mistake of leaving you once. It'll take more than a baby to make me leave again."

"Even if it's not yours?" I couldn't help but ask. I needed to know what to expect when the time came. Jack had already made his stance perfectly clear. And Raiden, I had a hard time seeing him leaving for that reason.

"There will be other children," Firestar

explained, pressing his lips to my forehead. "Mine does not have to be the first."

"And what of being Lord of the West? Whoever's child it is will gain that title," I reminded him with a frown. My father had made it very clear who would gain his kingdom and the only way I would was to have a child. Anybody's child.

Firestar scoffed. "You forget that I have a kingdom of my own to rule, and once my father has passed, I couldn't think of anything better than to combine the two. Then we will never be separated." He cupped my face in his hands and pressed his lips to mine in a chaste kiss. When he withdrew, he smiled. "Now, let's go see if there is a fuss to be made about."

Beaming up at him, I nodded.

We made our way out of the bedroom Jack's uncle had been kind enough to provide and knocked on Raiden's door. When no one answered, I frowned.

"Maybe they already went to the infirmary?"

Firestar shrugged. "We can at least go and see."

I tried to remember which way Lord Fafnir had told us the infirmary was and started that way. We only took one wrong turn before we found a large door at the end of a hallway. That had to be it.

"What do you think of our host?" Firestar asked as we approached the infirmary. "He seems to have less of a stick up his butt than our Jack."

My lips ticked up into a smile at his reference to Jack being ours, but I didn't comment. "He seems nice enough. Though, it's curious that he wasn't surprised by our arrival."

"Isn't that suspicious?" Firestar's brow crinkled.

I chuckled. "Not if what my studies have told me. A lot of the ice dragons have the sight."

Firestar's eyes widened, and his mouth gaped slightly. "Really?"

"Truly." I nodded before stopping at the door labeled 'Infirmary.' "Most of them can only see small spans of future though, and it's usually broken up too much to tell what is really going to happen."

"What good is that then?" Firestar scoffed. "I would think that would cause more confusion than good."

I shrugged. "I wouldn't really know. I've never met a seer and never wanted to. Knowing too much about one's future can cause more pain than its worth. Besides, can you imagine? Knowing when you or someone close to you will die?" I shook my head with a frown. "Too painful."

"Oh, I don't know," a soft feminine voice said as

the door to the infirmary opened. "I've found it to be quite useful in my field of work."

The woman who stepped out of the infirmary had pale hair like many of her fellow northerners. Jack's eyes were a light blue, but hers held practically no color at all, the irises barely distinguishable from the rest of her eye. She folded her hands in front of her, her white clothing a stark contrast to her dark skin.

"Hello," I said, offering my hand to her. "You must be the medic. I'm Maya, and this is Firestar." I gestured to the man at my side.

"I know." She took my hand in hers, her skin as cool as Jack's usually was. "I'm Trina."

Trina didn't try to squeeze my hand like some female dragons would. She simply shook it and let go before ushering us inside.

"Pleased to meet you." I glanced around the room. "Have the others arrived yet?"

There were several cots, but only a couple of them were occupied with sleeping patients though I couldn't see them since curtains separated each of them. Well, that was good. I wouldn't have to worry about their prying eyes.

Trina led us toward the back of the infirmary without responding to my question. Instead, she answered my question not with words, but by pulling back the curtain of the last partition, revealing Jack and Raiden talking quietly amongst themselves.

Well, that was certainly interesting. While I'd only been in the infirmary back home, the medics there were pretentious snots, thinking they knew more than anyone because they could heal. Trina didn't seem to share that same line of thought.

As we approached, the conversation between Jack and Raiden died off, and they both looked at me.

"Maya," Jack said, standing. "How are you feeling?"

I let him take me into his arms, seeking comfort in his embrace. "I'm fine. No more nausea." For now.

"And how's our fearsome warrior?" Raiden smirked, laughter in his eyes as he nodded toward Firestar. "Are you sure you are strong enough for this?"

Firestar growled, stepping toward Raiden. "I'm fine … or do you need proof, funny boy?"

Raiden's smile broadened. "I might just need that but not right now. After." He nodded toward where Trina stood by the bed.

Firestar followed his gaze and then relaxed. "After."

I exchanged a look with Trina who shook her head with a smile. Men.

"Please." She gestured toward the bed that sat up higher than the others in the infirmary. "Lay down."

I eyed the guys, my heart pounding in my chest. Swallowing thickly, I hopped up on the bed and inched myself down. My pulse raced in my ears, and a storm of emotions ran through me. Was I pregnant? Did I want to be pregnant? Oh god, what if I was? Could I really be a mother, especially with all the people who wanted me dead?

A warm hand grasped mine, and I glanced up to see Raiden smiling down at me. "Everything will be fine."

Licking my lips, I nodded and squeezed his hand. Jack and Firestar stood just behind him, there for me without crowding me. I felt like an animal on display as it was without them all looming over me.

"All right," Trina began, taking her place on the other side of me. "I'm going to lift your shirt just a bit. It's easier to do this if I'm touching your skin."

"Do what?" I asked a bit breathless as nerves began to kick in.

She gave me a reassuring smile. "I will focus my magic on seeking out another life. Then we will know if you are truly carrying."

"And you've done this before?" My nerves made my voice shake. I knew medics had all kinds of ways to know if someone was pregnant but usually it required more invasive procedures. I wished more than anything to be back on Earth and could just pee on a little stick. That seemed so much more humane than letting a woman I didn't know push her magic into me.

"Trina is our best medic," Jack answered for her. "She has healed many of our people and delivered most of them into this world as well. Maya," he said my name softly, brushing my hair away from my face, "you have nothing to fear from her."

I smiled up at Jack before nodding to Trina. "I'm ready."

Trina gave Jack an appreciative grin before moving my shirt up enough to place her hands on my stomach. Her hands were cool, and I jumped in place slightly. Trina's apologetic eyes met mine before she returned to her task.

Her fingers moved along my stomach, and a tingling sensation began to form. She stopped just below my belly button and pressed slightly, causing the tingling to increase sharply, and I gasped. My eyes widened as a second heartbeat filled my ears.

"Do you hear that?" Trina asked, her eyes still on my stomach.

"Yes," I breathed, amazed at the sound filling my ears. "I hear it."

Trina turned her eyes to look at me, a smile covering her lips. "That is the sound of your child's heartbeat. Congratulations."

So, overjoyed by the news, my doubts about the whole thing settled down to a dull roar. My lips spread out into a large grin, and I couldn't hold back the tears of relief. I was going to a mother. The concept caused so many mixed feelings that I had a hard time sorting them out.

One emotion was clear as day, though, as the men around me whooped and cheered, clapping each other on the back.

"Hey," I shouted over their self-congratulations. "I'm the one that's pregnant. How about a bit of attention over here?"

The men had the decency to look embarrassed before they began to crowd around me. Each of them took a turn to kiss me and express their happiness.

It was short lived though. I barely had a chance

to get off the table before the doors to the infirmary burst open, and several people clamored in.

"Trina!" one of the men shouted. "We need healing."

Trina ripped the curtain back and rushed out. Six men carried two bodies into the infirmary, bringing them right over to a set of beds. My men and I slowly approached from behind, not wanting to get in the way but too curious to just leave.

When I stopped at the end of the beds, it took a moment for me to realize what I saw. Two men lay bloodied and unconscious. Even with their faces barely recognizable through the gore, I knew exactly who they were.

Raiden's brothers.

4

The last time I'd seen Fujin and Raijin, the twins had stayed behind to hold off their mother's guards while we fled for our lives from the eastern palace. They were supposed to meet up with us later, but they never had.

Now I knew why.

"Fujin! Raijin!" Raiden cried out, trying to push through the crowd of men to reach his brothers. The agony in his voice made me ache for him. I could imagine how he felt. It had to be the same way I felt when I had thought he and Jack had been lost to me.

I started forward to stay by Raiden's side, but Jack's hand on my shoulder stopped me. Glancing up at him, he shook his head, and I held back.

There wasn't anything I could do for him right now. Not until we knew what we were up against.

"They're still alive, but barely," Trina explained as she looked over the twins' wounds. I couldn't see how she could tell that, I couldn't even see their chests moving. Their clothing had turned brown from the dried blood.

"Marcus! Corina!" Trina yelled. A man and a woman rushed into the room garbed in the same white uniform as Trina. They came to her side, ready to take orders.

Even if Jack hadn't assured me, I could tell Trina was far more competent in her role than many of the medics I'd met. She ordered the two around as she worked on cleaning and healing the wounds. Since there were two patients, Trina had to split her time between them, making the work a slow and grueling process.

Raiden stayed by his brothers, anguish in his expression until Trina announced, "Please clear the room, I can't do my job if you get in the way."

While I wanted to stay, there was nothing for us to do, and at the moment, it did just seem like we were in the way.

"She's right, we should let her work," I said, reaching out to Raiden. "Let's wait just over there."

I nodded to the door. He shoved my hands away from him with a watery snarl.

"No, I won't leave them again. This is my fault. I should never have left them."

Jack glanced at Trina who pressed her lips together in a thin line before nodding. "Fine, but stay out of the way and don't make a fuss. The rest of you can come back later when we have something new to report."

"Okay." Tears burning my eyes, I let Jack and Firestar guide me out of the infirmary, but I kept glancing back at Raiden. He was my funny guy. He always had a laugh and smile for me, but he didn't now.

"Trina knows what she's doing." Jack put pressure on my elbow, grabbing my attention. "If anyone can save them, she can."

I kept silent but inclined my head slightly. I didn't doubt the medic's abilities, but she couldn't help Raiden if they were beyond saving. He'd already lost his mother. I didn't know what would happen if he lost his brothers too.

"Why don't we go find something to eat?" Firestar suggested, glancing at Jack over my head. "I made you miss breakfast earlier. You must be famished, and you need to keep up your strength now more than ever."

Honestly, I couldn't think of food right then. My heart ached for Raiden, but I knew I had to eat. My hand touched my flat stomach, and I remembered the sound of the baby's heartbeat. He was right. I wasn't just eating for me anymore. There was another life I was responsible for now.

"Come," Jack said, taking my silence as agreement. "I'm sure the cook can whip something up to ease your mind. We have one of the best cooks in all Waesigar, and if I must say so, he makes one of the best raspberry tarts I've ever had."

"That sounds great." I forced a small smile though I didn't feel it. The guys had enough to worry about without having to worry about me losing it. I had to keep it together especially for Raiden. The last thing he needed right now was to see me worried too, that'd just make things harder on him. No. I had to be strong and take care of the baby. That's what he would want me to do.

Half an hour later, we were seated in the small dining room off the kitchen, though none of us were speaking. The cook, a particularly slim man named Carl, had brought us some of his famous raspberry tarts. I had nibbled at it to be polite but couldn't stomach it. My insides were in too much turmoil, thinking about what could be happening on the other side of the house.

"Not hungry or don't like it?" Jack asked, looking over at me as he took a small bite of his tart and chewed slowly.

"I… it's fine, I'm just, you know." I gestured toward the door. "Too anxious, I guess."

"It's fine, you don't have to lie about it, Maya," Firestar said, giving me a forced grin. "I never trust a thin cook either." He nodded at the half-eaten tart on his plate. "I don't even like it, I just didn't want Jack to feel bad since he talked them up so much, but then I realized I couldn't let you keep living in denial." He reached out and patted Jack's shoulder. "Sorry."

I couldn't tell what reaction he was going for because instead of getting annoyed, Jack simply raised an eyebrow at him.

"That's your sixth tart." Jack shrugged. "But I appreciate what you're trying to do." He sighed. "I'm worried too."

"It's amazing how quickly everything changes. I mean, we just found out Maya was pregnant, and…" Firestar trailed off as he turned his gaze went to the doors as if Raiden or Trina might appear at any moment.

"You're right," Jack said, and the sound of his voice brought my eyes back to him. "We should be celebrating the baby." He nodded to me. "Say, do you think it's a boy or a girl?"

"I, um, I don't know." I flushed. "I hadn't even thought about it."

"I would rather a girl," Firestar chimed in, but when I turned toward him, I found him still looking toward the door. "You know, rather a daddy's girl than a momma's boy and all that." He rolled his eyes. "We saw how well that worked." He paused. "I didn't mean it that way."

"Maybe we should go for a walk?" Jack suggested, standing from the table. "I can show you around the town. Some fresh air might do you some good."

I shook my head not following his lead. "I don't really feel like walking."

"Maya," Firestar started, his tone the kind he used when commanding his men, "you will make yourself sick wallowing. Best keep busy until we know there is something to worry about. Go with Jack. I'll come find you the moment they report anything."

"Are you sure?" I asked, anxiety eating at me. "What if something happens and I'm not here? Who's going to be there for Raiden? It's my fault his brothers got hurt in the first place." I shook my head, my face pinched in pain.

"Nonsense," Jack snapped. "You didn't force them to stay behind. They wanted to."

"But they wouldn't have had to if I had just done what their mother wanted. Maybe then Raiden wouldn't have lost her—"

"That wretched woman would have pushed her sons away in some form or another. Don't you dare blame yourself for her misdeeds." Jack growled, his eyes flashing with anger I rarely saw on his face.

I gripped the edge of the table as I tried to calm down. Jack was right as usual. It wasn't my fault Raiden's mother was a cold-hearted bitch. I couldn't have stopped her from being the way she was any more than I could stop my father. All I could do was worry about how I acted in response, and right now I needed some air.

"I think a walk might be a good idea," I said finally, standing from the table. Jack offered me his arm, and I readily took it before glancing over my shoulder to Firestar. "Coming?"

"Out there?" Firestar glanced out the window

and then shivered. "No, thank you. Besides," - he paused, reaching across the table and grabbing my neglected plate - "I missed breakfast too."

I rolled my eyes as Jack led me out of the dining room and down the hallway. We didn't get very far before we almost ran right into Raiden.

His eyes were down on the ground, his pace fast as he came down the hallway. The intense look on his face explained why he didn't see us or even smell us before we came into view.

"Raiden, everything okay?" I called before he could run us over.

Raiden's gaze shot up to me and his face softened. His pace increased, and when he was close, he scooped me up into his arms, burying his face in my neck. He inhaled deeply, almost crushing me to him.

"Mmm… you smell like raspberries." He didn't say it like he normally would have. No, the tone was all off, and it was obvious he was trying to hide his emotions. I didn't complain though, knowing he needed me.

Instead, I ran a hand through his dark hair and made a shushing sound while he composed himself. "It's all right. I'm here."

Eventually, his grip on me relaxed, and he

placed me back on my feet with a sigh. "Thank you, I needed that. Remind me next time to just leave when someone I love is being treated. It was worse watching them being healed because I couldn't do anything but stand there like an idiot. I should have just gone with you. I'm sorry."

"It's okay, Raiden," I said, smiling at him.

"Are they all right?" Jack asked, placing a hand on Raiden's shoulder.

Raiden nodded. "A bit worse for wear, but they will live. Trina gave them a sleeping drought, but they will be awake soon enough."

"How about you?" I grabbed his hand in mine. "Are you, all right?"

He gave me one of his lopsided grins. "You know me, nothing can keep me down."

To the outsider, those words would have been enough to put the subject to rest, but I knew better. He used that smile of his to hide his pain, his jokes to cover up the hurt. Raiden did a good job making those around him laugh and smile, but when it came to cheering himself up, he wasn't so good at it.

"We were about to go for a walk." I glanced at Jack, who nodded in agreement. "Would you like to join us? Maybe they will be awake by the time we return."

Raiden's face bunched up in thought before he sighed. "Sure, it can't be worse than waiting around here. Trina assured me it would be several hours before either of them will have the strength to tell us what happened, if they even woke at all today. I'm not going to do any good waiting by their bedside like an over-anxious wife."

I shot him an annoyed look, but let it go. If he needed to make jokes to make himself feel better, I wasn't going to deny him. Instead, I looped my arms through both of theirs and continued down the hallway.

"So, tell me about the village," I started, trying to distract all of us from the elephant in the room. "Are there many trades here? I mean there's so much snow, I can't see how you have any plants at all."

Jack snorted. "Just because we have limited resources doesn't mean we don't have the means to feed ourselves. We fish and hunt for meat. The plants we can't grow using heat lamps, we trade for with neighboring kingdoms." Jack paused, his lips pursed. "Well, we used to. Now that the East has been taken over, I'm not sure how that will affect our trade."

Raiden shook his head. "Don't worry about that. My mother might be a lot of things, but she is always a diplomat. She wouldn't chance angering the other regions because of internal issues. In fact, I doubt she will want it out that she has taken the throne. She'll probably make the people think my father is ill or something and not locked in the dungeons."

I didn't doubt that. Lady Nariko wouldn't risk losing her throne by letting anyone know she had committed treason. Especially since we were a patriarchy, and the rival lords wouldn't accept a female ruler no matter how she had taken the throne.

That said, as we exited Jack's home, I regretted it immediately. The cold air burned my skin, reminding me I didn't have a coat on. Jack, as usual, didn't seem bothered, but Raiden shivered beside me.

"Holy balls, it's cold." He rubbed his hands over his arms. "How do you stand it?"

Jack shrugged. "It doesn't bother me, but you, my dear, are expecting one. It won't do to have you catch a chill." He pulled me back inside and reached into a closet near the door. Pulling out a coat that must be for visitors, he held it out for me. "You shouldn't be out here without a coat."

"Hey!" Raiden called out. "What about me? I'm cold too."

Jack reached into the closet, pulled out another furred coat, and tossed it at Raiden. The lightning dragon barely caught it before it hit him in the face. Grumbling under his breath about cold hearts and icicles up butts, Raiden pulled his coat on.

"Ready?" Jack asked with a menacing grin, not in the least bothered by Raiden's comments.

"Always," Raiden responded before leading the way out of the house once more.

Jack and I trailed after him, even though Raiden probably had no idea where to go. It didn't take him long to stop and wait with a hand on his hip.

"What's taking you two so long." He rolled his eyes, gesturing for us to move along the path. "It's going to be annoying if I have to keep waiting so maybe you should just lead."

"You make an excellent point," Jack replied, not bothering to comment further. The ice dragon was surely the more mature of the two.

We walked between the houses down a road made of straw. Snow had been shoveled from the path to build small walls alongside. The burning wood smell was still there like before, but now it was accompanied by a sweet and spicy scent. My eyes searched for the source of the delectable aroma and found many more stalls than our first trek through town.

I was suddenly ravenous. Before I could make my stomach's demands verbal, something else came to my attention.

As we made our way to the heart of the town, people stopped and greeted Jack. They seemed genuinely happy to see him and many of them he knew by name.

"Remarkable," I murmured.

"What is?" Jack asked, turning away from the old man who had insisted on showing him his new grandchild.

I waved a hand around us. "That you know all these people." I couldn't imagine knowing everyone in my town, but then again, my father rarely let me mingle among the commoners. Hell, the only time I'd really interacted with them was when I'd snuck out.

"Of course," Jack replied with a lift of one shoulder. "I grew up here. Our community is a small one, and it takes a village to make sure everyone is cared for. I've even been scolded a time or two by the man we just saw."

"Really?" Raiden's brow rose clearly also finding the situation unusual.

"Do you always have so many foreigners?" I asked, pointing at a guy bundled up in a bright blue parka. While the ice dragons dressed as if it were a nice summer day, those like Raiden and I who were not used to the cold were bundled up to their ears, and it made them stick out like sore thumbs.

The thing was, there were almost as many ice dragons as there were those bundled up for the weather. Back home, we maybe had a dozen or so non-earth dragons living amongst us and rarely as many as this visiting. Sure, my father was strict on the comings and goings of those who don't belong, but this seemed excessive even to me.

"Uncle Fafnir does not believe turning people away because they are different is right. He believes, like most of us do, that if we are to survive as a species, we must welcome all."

"Aren't you worried about spies? Invaders?" Raiden's questions matched my own thoughts, and I was glad he'd voiced them because I'd been about to.

Jack shrugged. "Our region is hardly fitting for

anyone not of our kind. Those who come here usually have nowhere else to go."

"They could be unaligned," I reminded him.

"Even the unaligned sometimes need somewhere to call home." Jack stopped at a booth where they were selling hot nuts. He took a moment to speak with the vendor before pointing at me. The red-faced man took one look at me and grinned before handing Jack a bag of nuts.

"Here, be careful they are hot but delicious," Jack said as he came back over and offered them to me.

"Thanks." I blew on one before popping it into my mouth. The sweet and spicy scent I had noticed earlier filled my mouth. How they were able to combine both of them into one made my mouth water.

"You're welcome." He nodded to me for a second before continuing, "The unaligned are usually made up of outlaws and outcasts. But sometimes they are families who have no choice, and the wilderness is no place for children. Who are we to turn them away?"

"Because you aren't stupid," Raiden pointed out as he stole a nut from my bag. He popped it into his mouth right before his expression filled with pain. "Ow!" He spat the nut out, fanning his tongue.

Laughing at his antics, I held the bag out of his reach. "Now, who is the stupid one?"

Raiden's eyes narrowed right before he launched himself at me. I ran away, my bag of hot nuts clutched to my chest as he chased me. People looked on with amused interest but generally went about their business. Distracted by the onlooking crowd, I missed Raiden coming up on me until he knocked me off my feet. My back hit the cold ground with a thump, and my treat bag went flying, spraying hot nuts everywhere.

"I've got you now," Raiden smirked down at me, his hands finding my side and making me laugh and squirm. "Do you concede?"

"Never!" I shouted, struggling against him. He kept tickling my sides until I couldn't breathe and had to give up. "All right! You win. You're not stupid."

"That's what I thought." Raiden stopped tickling me and stood. As he helped me to my feet, I frowned at the ruined bag of nuts.

"You made me drop my nuts," I pouted, crossing my arms over my chest.

Raiden wrapped an arm around my waist and

pulled me close to his side. Whispering so no one could hear, he said, "That's okay. I have a better pair you can have later."

My face heated at his crude words, and I glanced around to make sure no one had heard him. Thankfully, everyone had returned to their own business.

As we walked back to where Jack stood, he gestured toward the spilled back. "Would you like me to get you some more?"

I shook my head, my face still aflame. "No, I think I've had all the nuts I can handle for now."

Raiden burst out laughing beside me before a coughing fit made him clear his throat. "Too true. Too true."

Jack raised an eyebrow at me, but when I didn't elaborate he just shrugged. "Ready to see more?"

"Sure, I think I can handle the cold for a few more minutes—"

"Jack, Maya, Raiden!" the medic, Marcus, called, interrupting me.

I spun on my heel to see him sprinting toward us, chest heaving with effort. He stopped when he reached us, his hands on his knees as he took a couple great gulps of air.

"What is it?" Raiden asked, his face filled with fear and worry. "Are my brothers okay?"

As I watched the medic struggle to breathe, all the anxiety from before came rushing back. The fear that Raiden would lose his family all in one go filled me to the brim. I wanted nothing more than for the medic's words to be positive, but I'd learned long ago not to hold my breath.

"No ... I mean yes. They're fine." Marcus shook his head, clearly insecure about his place. "In fact, they're awake. That's why I came. They need to speak to you right away!"

5

———

The infirmary doors banged against the walls as Raiden rushed inside. Jack and I trailed behind him, trying to get him to calm down. His brothers were healing. They didn't need him freaking out.

Firestar was with Trina at the end of Fujin's bed. Fujin and Raijin were still laying down, but their eyes were wide open as they watched their brother come storming over to them.

"Now, hold on a moment." Trina held her hand up to stop Raiden's approach. "They might be awake, but they are still weak. You can't overload them right now."

"They're my brothers," Raiden snarled, his eyes

wild as they flew over to his brothers before settling on the medic. "I just want to see them."

"Trina, it's fine," Fujin said weakly from his bed. Then, groaning the whole time, pushed himself up on his elbows. "He's just gonna keep pestering you until you let him talk to us. Besides, we have much to discuss." His brown eyes circled the room. "We all do."

Trina dropped her arm to her side, and though she was still frowning, she stepped to the side. Raiden wasted no time barreling past and knelt between his brothers. Grabbing their hands in his, Raiden searched their faces. I didn't know what he was looking for, but he seemed to have found it because the next thing I knew, he was smacking his brothers on the arms and yelling at them.

"What the hell were you two thinking? Never again! Never again will you put yourselves in danger like that," Raiden shouted, still banging on his brothers' arms, making them wince in pain.

Jack and Firestar shot over to Raiden, grabbing hold of the distraught dragon and pulling him back. Raiden fought against them, but they held onto him while Firestar whispered something in his ear that eventually made him calm down.

The pair let Raiden go hesitantly. It was as if

they expected him to jump at his brothers again. I understood Raiden's frustration. If it had been my sister Aeis lying there, I'd have been upset too. But his brothers were still healing, so giving them their well-deserved beating would have to wait until later.

"I'm fine." Raiden shoved at the guys' hands that reached out to him when he tried to approach the twins once more. "I'm sorry." He directed his apology to his brothers who watched him with growing amusement.

"It's all right," Fujin said with a lopsided grin. "We know crazy runs in the family. It was bound to be in one of us."

"That's right," Raijin chuckled. "They already had two perfect sons. As the youngest, it's only normal you would get the short end of the straw." His eyes darted down to Raiden's lower region as the twins chortled.

"Oh, like you are God's gift to the world," Raiden snorted, not at all bothered by their insults. Their relationship was so carefree. They were so at ease with each other, something I'd never had with my own sister. Aeis might be a lot of things, but she'd never openly teased me, at least not since we were children.

"You two have no room to talk as it is," Raiden

continued, pointing a finger at the two. "If you think I'm the less blessed of this family, our boy Jack would put you to shame."

It took me a moment to realize what Raiden had just implied before my face heated. I couldn't believe Raiden would say such a thing. The twins and Firestar looked at Jack as if trying to see beneath his clothing. The stoic dragon didn't so much as flinch but simply crossed his arms over his chest, his face as hard as marble.

"Nah, no way," Fujin scoffed.

After failing to find what he was looking for, Raijin turned his attention back to his younger brother and asked, "How do you know?"

Raiden opened his mouth to answer but was cut off by Fujin. "No, I don't want to know. Just the visual is bad enough."

They definitely had a different kind of relationship. I shook my head and couldn't help but smile. Strange as it was, they had the close kind of relationship I wished I had with my own sibling.

"Now, that we've decided who's got the bigger ... ego." Raiden glanced my way with a wink, making me roll my eyes, "what happened back home after we left?"

Raijin pursed his lips together before sighing.

"We dispatched the men who had come to take you out and then tried to fight our way to the courtyard."

"We wanted to clear a path for you to get out," Fujin explained.

"But the palace was swarming with men." Raijin shook his head in confusion. "If they had been our own, we could have talked them down, made them see reason, but these were men who we'd never seen before."

"Did you figure out who they were?" Firestar asked, stepping closer to the twins. "Who's helping your mother?"

"His name's Drac," Fujin growled. "He's a rich son of a bitch who lives on the eastern coast. Apparently, he is some distant cousin of my mother's."

"And just as ruthless," Raijin interjected with a scowl.

Since our arrival, I had stayed on the outskirts of the group, not wanting to get between Raiden and his brothers. Now, though, I needed to hear this. If we were going to save their kingdom and rescue Lord Shen, we needed all the information we could get.

"How many soldiers does he have?" Raiden

asked, taking a seat on the edge of Fujin's bed. "Do we have a chance?"

Fujin and Raijin exchanged a look, one I knew very well. They didn't want to say which meant it was bad, really bad.

They must have decided beforehand to let Fujin tell us the bad news because he shifted on his bed and braced himself for an attack.

"Just from what we saw at the palace," Fujin met Raiden's eyes, "thousands, maybe more."

Jack finally decided to put in his own opinion. "That doesn't make sense. There weren't that many when we escaped. There were maybe twenty or thirty men. I know, I fought them." He glanced at the others for confirmation.

"He's right." Firestar nodded. "They hadn't even thought to protect the city wall. You can't tell me they were all in the palace when we left."

"No," Raijin answered with a shake of his head. "They showed up later."

"We got out of the palace and were on our way to meet you when we encountered them," Fujin added, a haunted look in his eyes. "They came from the sky. We never saw them coming."

"That's how we found out about Drac and his relation to our mother, as well as his men," Raijin finished for his brother, too caught up by his own demons to say more.

"Then how did you get away?" Raiden asked, placing his hand on Fujin's hand. "Why aren't you dead?"

"Mother," Fujin spat. "She wanted to teach us a lesson, and try to convince us to take her side. With blood and pain."

"But that's where she made her vital mistake," Raijin menaced. "We don't respond well to threats, and it didn't take long for their guards to be lax enough for us to escape."

"And now here you are," I said with a sad sigh, wishing things could have been different. If only we had stayed behind with them, maybe they wouldn't have been captured. We could have saved them all the pain they had endured.

"Please don't blame yourself, Maya," Fujin's expression softened which only made me wrap my arms around myself tighter. "It wasn't your fault. We chose to stay behind."

"Exactly." Raijin nodded. "Our mother must have been looking for just the opportunity to take over the kingdom. She's always said our father was far too weak to rule and needed to show more power if he ever planned to gain respect from the other lords."

"And now you've not only lost your mother, but your father and kingdom as well." I sighed and ran my hand over my face. "It seems no matter where I go, something bad follows. Maybe I should have stayed on Earth like I had originally planned."

"Oh, Maya." Raiden stood from the bed and took my hands in his. "Like I've told you before, it's not your fault. Even Firestar's father being a total tool didn't happen because you came back."

Firestar placed a hand on my shoulder with a small smile. "I think my people would definitely agree with Raiden. It's only gotten better for them since you came through."

"But I didn't get your father imprisoned," I countered.

"We'll save my father, don't worry." Raiden wrapped his arms around me. I inhaled his scent, letting it soothe my worries. It didn't seem right that he was the one comforting me rather than the other way around.

"But how?" I protested. "Like your brother said, your mother has thousands at her beck and call, and we have a total of seven people against an army. It'd be suicide."

"Then you are going to need help." Lord Fafnir stalked in the room as only a member of the royalty could. His son, Tyrell followed at his side as well as his wife, Ingrid.

"Lord Fafnir," Raiden said with a nod. "We would appreciate any help you could provide, but I fear from what I've seen of your little village, your numbers would not be enough to save our father."

"No offense taken," - Lord Fafnir waved off Raiden's comment, - "and you are correct. We do not have the men to make a difference against your mother, but we can get them."

"Where?" Firestar asked, his brow furrowing. "There's not another village for miles."

Lord Fafnir smiled, patience in his eyes. "The winter games, of course."

Jack jolted, catching my eye. He didn't seem very happy with Lord Fafnir's suggestion, whatever it was he meant.

"What about the winter games?" Raiden asked, and this time Jack was not silent.

"Every year, we have a set of games. Three challenges to show an ice dragon's prowess, strength, and wisdom." Jack's jaw tightened as he explained it. The thing was, from what he'd said, I couldn't figure out why he was so upset about it, but now wasn't the time to ask.

"So, how are these games going to help us?" Fujin asked from his bed.

"Because in two weeks' time, some of the strongest men and women of the north will be headed here to participate." Lord Fafnir smirked. "That will be your chance to build your army."

"But why would they fight for us?" Raijin's suspicion was plain on his face. "Soldiers who fight because they are commanded to are less likely to succeed than soldiers who fight for a cause. While I don't wish to spit on your gracious offer, I just don't see how they will help us."

I had a hard time disagreeing with Raijin. We didn't want soldiers who would run if it suited them, abandoning us to be slaughtered. If we had gold to pay them, that would have been something, but none of us had anything with us that would make a difference.

Lord Fafnir laced his fingers in front of him as he approached us. "The thing you must understand is that our people were born to fight. Life in the north can become rather dull and uneventful when nobody wants to attack lest they freeze to death." He had a wicked grin on his face that said how satisfied he was with his impenetrable kingdom. "I'm sure there will be many who would kill for the chance to get out of the north and fight for a cause other than who gets the last piece of the raspberry pie."

Fafnir's son and wife laughed slightly at that, the only change in their faces since they arrived.

"It seems we have little choice." Raiden sighed, his arms tightening around me. I could tell how conflicted he was because I felt it too. I didn't like asking for help from people we didn't know, but we didn't have much of choice. If we ever planned to have any hope of saving Lord Shen, we'd need all the help we could get. Hopefully, it didn't come back to bite us in the ass.

6

———

Waiting for the games to begin was pure torture. It would be weeks before the other villages arrived and until then we had absolutely nothing to do but wait.

I hated waiting.

Lady Ingrid had offered me the use of her salon, a sitting room for ladies, to entertain myself but I'd declined, at first. After a few days of listening to the guys talk about fighting, I was ready to tear my hair out. I liked to train as much as the next dragon, but Earth had spoiled me. I needed variety.

Hence why I now stood outside the salon, wringing my hands in front of me. I'd never been one to hang out with other women. Not unless we were trying to rip each other apart on the training field. Back on Earth, Bianca had been one of the only females I had gotten close to, but that's because she was more interested in talking about herself than trying to find out all my secrets. Which I had plenty.

I worried that the moment I stepped in the salon the women would bombard me with questions. Questions I wasn't ready to answer.

Ready to turn on my heel and run back to my room, I jumped in place as the door swung open. Lady Ingrid stood in the doorway with a bemused look on her face.

"I thought I heard someone out here. Please come in." She stepped aside and gestured for me to enter.

Dropping my hands to my sides, I forced myself to smile though I was pretty sure it looked more like a grimace. I moved into the room and immediately felt like all their eyes were on me. There were at least a dozen other females in the room, and they were looking at me like I was a new toy they wanted to play with before discarding.

"Everyone," Lady Ingrid drew the attention of the room and placed a hand on my arm. "This is Maya. She's Jack's new mate." A chorus of murmurs followed, but if anything, the level of interest in me had heightened.

"Hello." I gave an awkward wave. Several women nodded in my direction and others muttered their hellos, but no one got up to greet me.

I stood in the middle of the room not sure what to do. Each of them seemed to be absorbed in their own activity. Some were even needle pointing. Gag me. Others were having tea. A shudder went through me as I remembered the last tea party I'd attended. That hadn't ended well for anyone.

"Maya, please come sit with me." Lady Ingrid took me by the elbow and ushered me toward a seat. She sat in the empty one next to me and offered me a teacup. I almost declined but then decided I needed something to do with my hands.

We sat there for a moment in silence. While most of the room's occupants had gone back to their chatter, every once in a while, they glanced my way. Still, I was happy I wasn't the only one in pants. There was a variety of attire in the salon. Hell, even Lady Ingrid had opted out of a dress today. One less thing to worry about.

When neither of us said anything, I decided to

break the ice. "You have a lovely home." Not the most original, but a girl had to start somewhere.

"Thank you," Lady Ingrid said with a small smile. "I can't tell you how overjoyed my husband and I are that Jack has brought you here. Even if under terrible circumstances." She frowned before drinking from her cup.

Taking a drink from my own, I realized it was real tea with caffeine and everything. Immediately, I set the tea to the side. Well, there went my distraction.

"Don't you like the tea?" Lady Ingrid asked, killing any chance I had at her not noticing. "I can ask for something else."

"Oh, no." I shook my head. "It's not the tea. Just I heard it's not good to drink caffeine when you're…"

"Oh!" Lady Ingrid covered her mouth as realization dawned on her. "I'm so sorry, dear. I completely forgot, how inconsiderate of me." She raised a hand, and a servant came over to her. "Please bring some herbal tea for Maya. Thank you." The servant nodded before hurrying away.

Shifting in my seat, I said, "You didn't have to do that. I don't want to be an inconvenience."

"Nonsense." Lady Ingrid waved me off. "You

are carrying my grandchild. The least I could do is make accommodations for you."

"You're pregnant?" A woman to my side with wide eyes and her white hair cut short asked her hand on my arm.

I nodded slightly. Not trusting myself not to put my foot in my mouth.

"How wonderful," she cried out and sighed dreamily. "Oh, I remember when I had my darling, Victor. It was the happiest day of my life."

"I'm surprised you remember," another woman a few seats away snorted. "Aren't you pushing three hundred and twelve?"

"Why you cheeky–" the other woman started but was interrupted by Lady Ingrid.

"Ladies. This is about the future generation, not you." She shot them a sharp look before turning back to me. "So, tell me. How are you feeling? Any sickness yet?"

I didn't bother to try to explain that the child might not be Jack's, I'd found some acceptance with them and didn't want to kill my upward trajectory.

"A bit." I flushed as all eyes watched me. "I mean, I've been sick a few times and seem to be irritated a lot more than usual."

The ladies around me laughed together as if

what I'd said was the funniest thing they had ever heard. If so, they needed a life.

"Oh, dear." Lady Ingrid patted my hand. "Just you wait. This is only the beginning. Those mood swings will get even worse." She paused for a moment and then her lips broke out into a broad smile. "But at least, you have three strapping men to take care of some of those more intense ones instead of just one."

A chorus of swoons followed Lady Ingrid's words though I wasn't a hundred percent sure what she was talking about. Having three guys to irritate you didn't seem like a good thing to me.

Seeming to notice my confusion, the lady next to me leaned in close. "She means when you start to need more attention in the bedroom."

My eyes widened. Lady Ingrid seemed like such a prim and proper woman. Not someone who discussed sex with her girlfriends. It seemed I had misjudged her.

"Tell me," the same woman started, "The big one, what's his name."

"Firestar," I provided.

"Is he proportionate in all areas?"

It took me a second to figure out what she was asking before my face heated. Was she seriously asking me how big Firestar's dick was? From the eager look on her face and the way everyone else seemed to lean in to hear my answer, I'd have to say yes. Yes, she was.

Not believing I was having this conversation, I answered, "Yes."

The women tittered about me, each gushing about their own lovers. While weird, I found the women's company to be comforting. If I closed my eyes, I could almost imagine myself back on earth just chatting with Bianca as she recounted her wild sexcapades.

A knock on the salon's door drew everyone's conversations to a halt. Raiden's dark head peaked in, and the women began to whisper amongst themselves. Not bothered by the attention he was getting Raiden entered the room and smiled.

"Good afternoon, ladies." His brilliant smile caused more than one of the women to blush, and I forced myself not to roll my eyes. The flirt.

Searching me out, Raiden came to a stop in front of me. Turning to Lady Ingrid briefly, he said, "I hope you don't mind if I whisk my mate away for a little while. I promise to bring her back in one piece."

"Oh no. Go ahead, whisk away." Lady Ingrid smiled behind her cup.

With Lady Ingrid's permission granted, Raiden took my hand and brought me to my feet. I could still feel the eyes of all the women on us even after we were back in the hallway.

I let Raiden lead me away for a few minutes before pulling him to a stop. "What was so important you needed to whisk me away?" I smirked at the wording. Really, I wasn't some damsel in distress.

Not seeming to care who saw, Raiden backed me up against the wall of the hallway and pressed his lips to mine. Mouth devouring mine, I gripped his shirt in fear I'd melt into a puddle on the floor.

After my panties were good and soaked, Raiden ripped his mouth away from mine with a hot look. "That's what."

He grabbed my hand once more and started down the hallway, our pace increased from before. This time though, I was in as much of a hurry as he was. Each step caused a delightful friction between my thighs and I was almost crying by the time we reached our rooms.

"Your room or mine?" Raiden asked. When I

shook my head, he shoved my bedroom door open. "Yours it is."

I'd barely gotten in the room before Raiden was on me again. He grabbed my hips and pulled me tightly against him, the hard evidence of his arousal pressed into my stomach. I ground against him without thinking causing him to growl.

"I've been thinking of getting you naked all day," Raiden admitted, his hands cupping my butt.

"Oh yeah?" I gasped. "All that talk of swords and blood make you hot and bothered?"

Raiden snorted. "No, the way you ate that whipped cream confection this morning did it. You really know how to tease."

I frowned. He couldn't possibly be talking about the whipped cream from this morning's breakfast. I'd had a crepe filled with fruit that had been to die for. Apparently, I had been so engrossed in my food I hadn't noticed anyone watching me.

"I assure you if I had been teasing I hadn't meant to be." I paused and groaned as he had my shirt over my head and my breasts in his palms within seconds. "But I think I should more often now."

With a fierce growl, Raiden jerked his shirt over his head before backing me up toward the bed.

Hooking his fingers into my pants, he pulled them over my hips before nudging me onto the bed. It took him a moment longer to take my boots off before he relieved me completely of my clothes. His clothing went next leaving him utterly bare.

My mouth watered in anticipation, and I reached for him, but he ducked out of my grip and knelt between my legs. His fingers gripped my thighs and held them apart as he dived into my heat. I grabbed the back of his head with one hand while the other clawed at the bed beneath me. His mouth teased and lapped at me until I was just on the edge before he pulled back, making me cry out in frustration. When I had almost lost my orgasm all together, he started again.

"Raiden, for the love of god!" I cried out when he denied me my release for the third time. "Stop with the torture, would you?"

"Say please."

"Pretty please with gobs of raspberry tarts on top!" I tugged at his hair in an effort to get him to begin again, but he only chuckled at my antics.

Much to my chagrin, he didn't immediately go back between my legs. Instead, he stood to his feet and moved across the room. Confused and turned on by the sight of him long and hard, I started to get off the bed.

"Don't move." He held a finger up before my feet could touch the ground. I quickly stopped moving and waiting anxiously for his return. He found the bottomless bag and began to rummage through it. When he came back, he had rope in his hands.

"What's that for?" I asked an eyebrow raised.

"Put your hands together," Raiden commanded in that alpha tone of his that made a shiver of delight run through my body. Doing as he told me, I clasped my hands in front of me. With deft hands, he quickly had the rope wrapped around my wrists. The material of the rope was rough but not so much that it bit into my skin. He'd tightened it enough that I couldn't move more than just my hands, my wrists securely trapped.

"Get onto the bed." There was that tone again, my inside gushed. I struggled to do as he commanded but found my bound hands made it hard to manage. Seeing my plight, Raiden lifted my legs and helped me onto the bed. He climbed on after me, taking the extra bit of the rope and dragging my arms up above my head.

With my arms secured above my head, I tested

them out, trying to get them loose but I was utterly trapped. Excitement filled me with what he would do to me next. Raiden had always been a bit of a dominant in the bedroom, but we hadn't gone so far as to use restraints before.

"Are you, all right?" Raiden asked as he settled in front of me. His eyes were searching my face, probably for any signs of discomfort or rejection. A big part of our play was about making sure I was comfortable. He never forced me further than I wanted to go but always strived to push my limits.

Nodding my head, I leaned back against the pillows; my arms pulled tight above me. My legs fell open on their own as Raiden moved closer to me. I hoped he'd continue what he had started but instead his mouth found mine. Tongues tangled, he dominated my mouth like he did everything else in bed never once letting me take the lead or become complacent.

When he released my mouth, my neck stretched to follow him before I couldn't move much more because of the ropes. Raiden didn't seem to notice my frustration and moved his lips down my neck and along my chest. He sucked my nipple into his mouth, one of his hands cupping the other one. My hips bucked off the bed, and I tried to get closer to him, but it seemed like the more I tried to get close to him the more he backed away.

Letting go of my breast with a smirk, I wished I had my hands back so I could smack him. My snarl of annoyance quickly turned to a gasp of pleasure as his fingers found their way into my slick heat. He thumbed my nub as he dipped first one and then two fingers inside of me.

Raiden moved at a maddeningly slow pace, making my release burn as it came up, but still, he didn't let me have it. I found myself utterly empty as he removed his hands from me completely. Ready to curse him out, using a few choice words I'd learned from Bianca, all I got out was fuck before he pushed into me.

No longer teasing, Raiden gripped my hips in almost a biting hold as he drilled himself into my insides. They clenched tightly around him as I gasped and moaned. I tried to grab him, to have something to hold onto but my hands were bound still, and all I could do was take what he gave me.

Which he did splendidly.

Eyes flashing gold, Raiden gave me a feral grin, his canines seeming longer than usual and danger-ously sharp. Seeing him like that should have scared me, but it only ended up making me finally come apart. Not giving me a second to catch my breath, Raiden kept going until he found his release and the roar that he let out shook the room.

Too tired to question it too much, I put Raiden's strange behavior to the back of my mind to think about later.

Raiden reached up and untied me, the circulation rushing back to my wrists making them tingle. He rubbed them gently with a satisfied grin on his face.

Letting him take care of me, I grinned. "So, whip cream, huh?"

The weeks that followed dragged on. By the time the winter games were upon us, we were all feeling tense, most of all me.

"What you are feeling is completely normal." Trina gave me a sympathetic look that made me want to punch her. How dare she be so nice to me?

Irritation pricked at me like an angry bitch, or rather dragon, waiting to rip someone's head off. My emotions had been going haywire the last few days, and I'd taken it out on the guys more than once.

Hence why I was currently sitting in Trina's office. Pretty Trina who didn't have a parasite growing inside of her making her feel like utter shit. Why did I want to be pregnant again?

Oh, yes. My father demanded it and who was I, as his daughter, to refuse? Screw him and the whole freaking kingdom.

"So, it's normal for my breasts to hurt, to throw up everything I eat, and to have this burning need to destroy something? That's normal?" I scoffed, disbelief in my voice.

Trina, the patient woman that she was, set down the clipboard she had been scribbling on and approached me. "Yes, and a lot more. Be prepared for rapid mood swings. Swelling. Even an overactive sex drive."

I snorted at that. Sex was the last thing on my mind right now. I felt disgusting and irritated all the time. The guys had started to treat me like a ticking time bomb ready to explode at the drop of a hat, and after kicking Raiden out of my bed more than once, none of them had broached the subject of sex.

Thank fuck.

Turning my attention back to Trina, I sighed. "So, when can I expect it to stop? Before the baby actually arrives, I hope?" I raised a brow daring to have a twinkling of that emotion inside of me.

Trina smiled and patted me on the arm. "Every woman's pregnancy is different. Most only are sick during the first trimester. Others are sick the entire length of the pregnancy."

My nose wrinkled in irritation. "So, you're saying I'm screwed? And not the good kind."

Laughing at my words, Trina shook her head. "You can eat crackers or another bland food to help the sickness. If you get heartburn, sleep reclined. As far as the irritability, try tea. They should have some peppermint or chamomile tea in the kitchens. It should make you and your men happier."

"Make them happier? They did this to me!" I frowned at the suggestion. "Sorry. Thanks, I'll try that." I hoisted my stupid body tom its stupid feet and made my way out of the infirmary in hopes of finding those things.

The guys had left me to my own devices today. They'd been too excited to see the arriving representatives from the outlying villages than to deal with me. I'd have gone out to watch as well, but my nose - like the rest of me - had gone haywire. The last time I went outside just the smell of the cooking nuts I had loved so much the first few days we arrived made my stomach turn. I wondered how many other things that I loved would I lose before this pregnancy was over.

"Hey," Firestar started when he came around

the corner and saw me. His eyes darted around me almost like he was searching for an escape path. When he found none, he asked cautiously, "How are you?"

I shrugged. "I just saw Trina, and she suggested a few things to make me less ..." I gestured to my stomach with an exaggerated movement. "Just less."

"Good. Good." Firestar nodded, and my eyes were drawn to his hair.

"Did you cut your hair?" I cocked my head to the side. The red hair I loved had grown since our time together, curling at the base of his neck. I loved to bury my hands in it while we made love. The same with all the guys. Who knew I was such a hair girl?

Now though. Now it was barely an inch long.

Firestar touched his head and gave a nervous chuckle. "Oh, yeah. It was getting long, and if I'm going to participate in the games, I didn't want to have to worry about it."

"But I liked it long," I pouted, fiddling with the end of his shirt. "Why didn't you ask me first?" I felt the first prick of tears that I knew would follow an epic breakdown. Another of the pleasant side effects of pregnancy.

"Oh no, Maya. I'm sorry," Firestar shushed,

pulling me into his chest and running his hand through my hair. "You're right, I should have asked. I didn't know you liked it so much."

"Neither did I," I cried into his chest. My face heated and my nose became stuffy. I'd never been a pretty crier, and with my hormones out of whack, it was a million times worse. Several people walked past us as I bawled my eyes out about something so silly, even I couldn't believe I was crying.

When my tears finally subsided, I pulled away from Firestar with a huff. "Well, that's getting old fast. I'm sorry, I got your shirt all wet." I picked at his shirt where it had become thoroughly soaked.

"It's fine." Firestar gave me a small smile, not even looking at his shirt. "Now, where were you headed off to? Maybe I could walk you?"

My lips twisted into a frown. "Why are you being so nice?"

Firestar frowned. "What do you mean? I'm always nice."

"No, you are surly, and anytime a woman cries, you run in the other direction. What gives?"

Sighing, he ran a hand over his face. "The others and I are trying to be more ... understanding."

"Understanding?" I drew out, placing my hands

on my hips and shifting my weight to one foot. "How do you need to be more understanding? Because I'm carrying one of your offspring, and it's slowly driving me mad?"

Firestar winced as my voice raised to a shout. Placing his hands on my arms, he moved them up and down in soothing strokes. "Please calm down."

"Don't tell me to calm down." I jerked away from him and snarled, "Your child is turning my body against me!" I spun on my heel and stomped away from him. Before I got more than five feet, I stopped and realized I was going the wrong way. Turning back, I hissed, "The kitchens are this way, not that you care." I shoved past him and around the corner he had arrived from. I half expected him to follow me, but when he didn't, my shoulders slumped, and regret filled me.

What the hell was wrong with me? I'd cried about something silly and yelled at Firestar all in the manner of a few seconds. I didn't care what Trina said, this couldn't be normal, but if tea would help, well, I'd drink all of it.

Later, I found myself four cups of chamomile tea deep and with an urgent need to pee. After I relieved myself, I sat back down at the table the kindly cook had been nice of enough to place another cup of tea on.

Trina had been right. I did feel better but worse at the same time. I didn't know if I was going to survive this pregnancy without killing one of the guys or even myself for that matter. God forbid I get postpartum depression, then no one would be safe.

"There you are," Raiden said as he sat down beside me. "I haven't seen you all day. Are you, all right?"

"I wished people would stop asking me that," I growled into my cup as I took another large swig. I wondered if drinking, so much tea could have the opposite of the intended effect because just seeing Raiden's face made me mad.

"Well, if you aren't going to talk, I will," Raiden said as he motioned for the cook. "Is it possible that you might have some of those famous tarts? I'm starving."

Carl smiled broadly. "You are in luck! I just pulled some out of the oven for this little lady. I'm sure there is enough to share."

As Carl wandered back into the kitchen, I muttered, "Traitor." I thought Carl and I had a special relationship, the kind where he brought me tea and sweets and didn't ask stupid questions. Now he was giving my sweets away. Guess love was fickle that way.

"So, the preparations are done," Raiden continued as if I had asked. "I can't say a lot about Jack and his people, but they sure know how to hold a contest. This is going to be one monstrous event. I can't wait to participate."

"Oh, joy." I rolled my eyes as I drained my cup. "Maybe during that time, you can remember why we really came here for? Like your father?"

The excitement in Raiden's eyes died, and I instantly felt guilty. "Sorry," I rushed to say, setting my cup down harder than I meant to. "I don't know what's come over me."

I did, but he didn't need to worry more than he already was. A pregnant lover and a family under siege had to make it hard to sleep at night. I knew it did for me.

"No, you're right. We should be focusing on what we came here for, not on some silly competition." He paused as Carl came out with the plate of tarts. The smile on his face was forced as he thanked him, but didn't touch his plate. "From what I can see, there are quite a few men and women who could help our cause. I hope that Lord

Fafnir is right when he said they were itching for a fight."

"I'm sure they are," I reassured him before I snagged a pastry and took a bite. I closed my eyes as I moaned in delight when the raspberry filling touched my tongue. After I swallowed and opened my eyes, Raiden was staring at me. "What? Do I have something on my face?" I touched my mouth expecting there to be something there but came back empty.

Raiden leaned forward and swiped his thumb across the bottom of my lip before popping it into his mouth. My eyes followed his movements as he slowly removed the digit from his lips. "Delicious."

Licking my lips, something I thought would be gone the whole pregnancy stirred within me. "Yeah," I breathed, a delightful ache burning at the junction of my thighs. "They really are."

Taking my chin in his fingers, he angled my face up before capturing my lips with his own. My hand came up and tangled in his hair, pulling him closer as he lay siege to my mouth. He tried to release me, but I followed him until I ended up in his lap. Our kissing slowed to a small brushing of lips before we withdrew to breathe.

"Tastes even better on you." Raiden smirked,

his arms wrapped around me, pulling me close. "I'm glad you are feeling better. I'd hate you to spend this entire time miserable. My mother told me about when she was pregnant with my brothers and me." He shook his head, a frown on his gorgeous lips. "If yours is even half as bad as hers, I fear we may just have to put you on the battlefield. At least that might scare off some of my mother's men."

"Hey!" I shoved at his chest. He laughed, and I couldn't help but break into a smile myself. "I don't think I'm that bad. It could be worse."

"Yes, it could be. But remember," he pressed his forehead against mine, "no matter how bad you get, I will always be there. All of us will be."

"Really?" I asked, genuinely needing the extra assurance. "Even when I'm fat and can't see my feet?"

"Especially when you are fat." Raiden smiled, putting his hand on my still flat tummy. "Even when you need us to carry you because your wings can't handle your magnificence."

"Haha, very funny." I poked at him with a smile. "You think you are so smooth, don't you?"

Raiden lifted a shoulder. "I try. Now," - he slid me off his lap and stood to his feet - "why don't we go check on the others? I'm sure they are dying to see you like I have been."

I snorted. "I doubt it. Firestar already had to endure my weeping spell, and then I blew up on him. I think he'd be rather happy if I stayed away."

"Nah," Raiden said, swiping his tart off his plate as we started toward the door. "Firestar's a big manly man. He wouldn't be scared of little ol' you."

I chuckled and leaned into his embrace. We walked through the halls toward the exit, chitchatting about what we might expect in the next few days. We stopped right before the house's entrance as my stomach rumbled. Raiden smiled at me before handing over the tart he had only taken a few bites of.

Then the waterworks happened again.

"Maya," Raiden cooed, tilting my chin up to him. "What's wrong?"

"You gave me your tart," I sniffled.

"Yes, I did. You need it more than me. You have a baby growing in you after all." He grinned and rubbed my back.

"But you were so looking forward to it. It's not right that I should have it." I almost shoved it back at him, but my stomach rumbled once more.

"See!" Raiden laughed. "Our child is hungry.

Feed it. I can get another later. I'm sure when I tell Carl how the mean pregnant lady stole it, he will be sympathetic to my plight."

My lip ticked up in a snarl. "Just for that, I will eat it." I dug into the tart with a ferocious growl that turned into a moan of pleasure. I couldn't even be mad with this much deliciousness in my mouth.

Raiden laughed and handed me my coat as he put on his. "Come along, my vixen. Let's see what games they have in store for us today."

"But I want to compete!" I whined for the millionth time as the guys stood around with stern expressions. I didn't see what the big deal was. It was just a game. Not real-life battle which I had already been in, recently.

If I was fine then while pregnant, I didn't see how fighting now that I knew I was would make a difference. If anything, it would make me more careful. Besides, I could use the exercise. All those raspberry tarts were starting to show.

"No," Firestar snapped, "and that is final. You are pregnant. You can't put yourself in danger just for some games."

"But I can take care of myself," I argued,

leaning forward with my hands on my hips. "I've handled myself fine in plenty of fights."

"But that was life or death," Jack pointed out, always the reasonable one. "This isn't. So, to risk yourself just to prove something is simply irrational."

"I'm just supposed to sit on the sidelines watching you have all the fun like a good little mate?" I snarled and stomped my foot. "No way!"

"You are being difficult on purpose," Raiden growled, the exasperation plain on his face.

I scoffed and waved a hand. "Yeah, because I woke up this morning deciding that I wanted to make your lives as miserable as possible. I have better things to do, like trying not to throw up everything I eat."

Rolling his eyes, Raiden sighed. "You can't blame everything on being pregnant. Besides, you being pregnant is our whole point exactly."

I opened my mouth to reply but closed it with a huff. I didn't have a quip for that one. So, I did what any mature, rational adult would do. Name called.

"Well, you are a stupid jerk face!"

That only made the guys groan and facepalm.

Unfortunately, our argument was beginning to

draw a crowd, something none of us really wanted. The guys tried to usher me back inside, but I shoved them away, not wanting any of them to touch me with their prejudiced hands.

Firestar's eyes lit up with anger. "Maya Rose, you are acting like a child."

"Then maybe you should stop treating me like one," I snapped back, trying to push my way through the guys and back to the sign-up booth.

They had set up the village square for what would be a glorious week of fighting and festivities, and for the first time in weeks, I was genuinely excited.

All I had experienced since I came back to Waesigar were attempts on my life and the ever-present pressure to get pregnant. Now that I finally was pregnant, and there were no assassins in sight, I planned to get my fun on.

It would have been great if everyone else had been on board too. The guys had all been talking about which game they would compete in, but when we got to the sign-up tent, they totally freaked out.

I didn't know what the big deal was. It wasn't like any of the events were real. Brawling, an in-flight race, and finally a hunt through the woods.

Sure, I could see how they would want me to stay out of the fighting, but I didn't see how flying or running through the woods could hurt me. They were just being overprotective, not that Firestar or the others would see it that way.

No longer trying to argue the point, I tried to dodge around them, but they were always one step ahead of me, blocking my path. Finally, tired of the guys treating me like a child, I turned on my heel and stomped back toward Lord Fafnir's house. I heard boots crunching in the hay-strewn streets behind me but didn't turn around to see who followed me.

When I arrived at the house, I attempted to slam the door behind me, but a big hand caught it. Firestar pushed through the door, and his large form loomed over me. Not to be intimidated, I glared right back at him.

Shutting the door behind him, Firestar crossed his arms over his chest as if his massive muscles would make a difference.

"You are being unreasonable," he calmly stated, which I knew meant he was just moments from blowing up. The calm before the storm and all that.

But my mouth didn't seem to care. I shoved a finger into Firestar's chest and bared my teeth at him. "You are the one acting like an overbearing asshole. You and the rest of you jerks treat me like I'm going to break. I'm pregnant, not made of glass!"

"Did you forget that not only Raiden's mother but your cousin wants you dead?" Firestar practically shouted at me, stepping forward, so I had no choice but to step back or get run over. "Or that if anything happened to our child that you would lose your leverage over your father?"

I frowned at his logic, my anger wilting slightly. "What does that have to do with anything? They don't know where we are. What makes you think they would find me just because I'm competing?"

"We don't know that they don't know where you are," Firestar growled, grabbing me by the arms. "There could be spies all over this place. As far as we know, one of the warriors that came in for the games could be one of Lady Nariko's men or even Ned's. You heard Lord Fafnir about vetting their visitors. There's no telling who he let in." He took a deep breath, trying to push down his annoyance with our host's lax admittance standards. "Hell, for all we know, every last one of them could be trying to murder you in your bed."

"Then maybe we shouldn't have come here," I

countered, getting impatient with the whole ordeal. "In fact, it seems like nowhere is safe for me. Maybe you should all take your chances on your own, and I'll just go back to Earth. There are plenty of single mothers there. I'm sure I'd be fine all by myself."

Firestar threw his hands up in the air and let out a frustrated roar. "Don't you hear yourself? Has this child muddled your brain so much that you can't see sense right in front of you?"

"This child?" I screeched, my eyes going wide. "This child that one of you put in me? This child that has my body in turmoil and has none of you wanting to touch me? You mean that child?"

"Is this what this is about?" Firestar scoffed and shook his head. "You think we don't want you anymore?" Before I had a chance to respond, he scooped me up and threw me over his shoulder.

"What do you think you are doing?" I beat at his back and kicked my legs. "Put me down, you savage. I can walk just fine."

Smack. Red hot pain seared through my backside as Firestar's hand found its mark.

"Quiet down," he growled, the feel of it rumbling through his chest and vibrating against me as we bumped along. Ridiculously delicious tingles spread through me from that vibration.

No, I was not going to let myself get turned on by this.

"Where are you taking me?" I tried once more to get some answers. "I have to sign up for the games."

"No, you don't." Firestar simply stated and then added, "I've found the cure for what ails you."

I snorted. "Oh, really? And what's that?"

Firestar shifted me a bit more roughly than needed as he rounded a corner, and I punched him in response. "You have been nothing but a pain in the ass the last two weeks, and I've had enough of it."

"Well, excuse me for being hormonal. You try having something growing inside of you some time and tell me how fun it is," I spat out as my eyes found the familiar hallway. We were heading back to our rooms. Why?

"If I could trade places with you, I gladly would. Then at least, I wouldn't have to listen to your harping, but as it is, I can't. So, I have something far more effective to settle your raging dragon."

I rolled my eyes and leaned on my elbow. "Please do enlighten me."

He stopped before a door, swinging it open, so it

slammed into the wall. With a few quick strides, he was across his bedroom. He dumped me onto the bed. I bounced on the mattress for a second and came up scowling.

Firestar closed and locked the door behind us before stalking toward the bed. The intense predatory look in his eyes had me backing up to the far side, and when he reached for me, I tried to scramble away, but he latched onto my ankle and dragged me back across the mattress. I screamed as he pulled me flush against him, beating at his chest.

"What are you going to do to me?" My voice came out breathless as I said it, half from arousal, the other from fear of the unknown. I knew Firestar would never truly hurt me but the threat that he just might just couldn't be dispelled.

"Giving you what you need. What we both need," Firestar answered before putting me over his lap like a disobedient child. Without warning, my pants were jerked off my butt, baring my cheeks to the room. When I realized what he was about to do, I tried to scramble off of his lap, but his arm came down over me, keeping me in place.

I was still trying to get free from him as I growled, "I can't believe you are really going to do this."

"Quiet or it will be worse," Firestar rumbled, his hand caressing my butt cheeks. Anticipation filled me as I waited for what I was sure to happen next. "Unless you'd like me to stop?" When I didn't immediately respond, he nodded. "That's what I thought."

The first slap of his hand against my cheek startled me. The stinging made me cry out. I tried to wiggle away, but Firestar held me fast, his hand rubbing the spot he had just hit. I wasn't prepared for the second swat any more than the first, and it ripped a pained gasp out of me. This time though, when Firestar's hand soothed my inflamed skin, his fingers dipped between my thighs. As his fingers stroked me, I realized I was already good and ready for him.

What the ever-living fuck?

I'd never considered myself someone into pain. Even Raiden - who was the kinkier of the three - hadn't used pain in our pleasure. He had more of a dominance kind of thing going on. Tying me up, blindfolds, commanding me around, those kinds of kinks. But now that I'd started to experience it, a mixture of emotions welled up in me. Surprise and excitement overwhelmed me to the point where when the next hit came, I craved it.

Now with each smack of his hand, Firestar rotated sides and teased my folds endlessly before the stinging sensation came again. When we reached five hits, I thought he might never stop, but then, as suddenly as he put me on his thighs, he had me back on the bed.

I winced as my backside hit the comforter, still stinging from Firestar's punishment, and watched as he undid his pants. My legs spread on their own, eager to take him in, but were caught when I realized my pants were still on. I reached for my boots, untying them as fast as I could, but before I could pull my pants down the rest of the way, he caught my hands and shook his head.

"Leave them on," Firestar commanded, one hand stroking his length, something that attracted my full attention, while the other held my legs in his grasp. He was already hard and long, the tip glistening in his arousal.

I licked my lips, and all the pain in my butt seemed to go to the back of my mind.

I let him drag me toward him, curious to what he had planned. Angling me to the side, he kept my legs pressed together, trapped beneath his arm, as he slid into me. I gasped at the fullness, the position making him feel much larger than he was.

Briefly, I wondered if Raiden's comments from before had caused this but quickly forgot about that when he withdrew only to push back in, making me cry out. Angled sideways, Firestar had complete control. My hands clung to the sheets beneath me as he stroked deep inside of me. The combination of the spanking I'd received mixed with his brutal thrusts and my lack of recent sex made my release come all too soon.

I cried out in pleasure as Firestar continued to take me. As I came down from my high, my pants were ripped away, and he maneuvered me onto my knees.

"Do you know," Firestar panted as he moved inside me once more, "how worried we are about you?"

"You are?" I gasped and groaned in response, trying to crane my head to see him.

Firestar's hand reached out and wrapped my hair in his fist, arching my neck to just this side of uncomfortable. "If anything happened to you, we couldn't forgive ourselves." He thrust his hips against me, grunting as he spoke. "Everyone wants you dead, and you can't be bothered to take precautions. Do you want to drive us mad?"

"No," I cried out as he hit a particularly sensitive place inside of me. I tried to say more, but he had adjusted his thrusts so that he hit that spot over and over. My vision started to blacken as my second release hit me. Heart racing, I feared I might just pass out from the sensations.

"I love you, Maya. We all do." Firestar grunted against me, his words coming out in pants.

"I love you all too," I barely choked out.

Firestar didn't say anymore but released my hair and focused entirely on driving me into oblivion. My pregnancy had made me even more sensitive than before, so when my orgasm to hit me, it hit hard. My mind spiraled, and my breath caught. All I could get out before I passed out was, "Oh fuck."

9

I had a silly, sated smile on my face as Firestar and I walked to dinner hand in hand. The fire dragon had been right. That had been exactly what I needed to get out of my slump.

My body felt light and floaty, not sick and disgusting like before. Any irritation I felt earlier that day seemed like a bad dream. I'd have to remember that for the future, though - I winced - maybe not so much the spanking part. My backside still stung.

"Hey, you're back!" Raiden greeted as we approached the main dining hall. Usually, we dined in the smaller one by the kitchen since there were fewer of us, but since so many people had shown up for the games, there were too many to fit inside.

I beamed at Raiden as Firestar allowed me to go into the lightning dragon's arms. A familiar stirring lit in my belly as his scent filled my sense. Again? Seriously, Trina hadn't been kidding about the increased libido. Or maybe it was because I hadn't been with any of them in weeks.

That said, I missed more than just sex with my guys. I missed curling up next to them, inhaling their scents as I fell asleep. I missed waking up next to them, their arms wrapped tight around me, making me feel safe and secure. If we hadn't been in public, I would have thrown myself at Raiden. I craved his touch that much.

"It looks like Firestar had the cure to what ailed you." Raiden chuckled as he directed me to one of the many wooden tables in the hall.

I flushed and ducked my head at his words, hoping no one heard him as I muttered, "Yes, I'm sure I'll need another dose tonight. Would you like to help?"

Raiden's arm slipped from my shoulders to caress my butt. "I'd be more than happy to administer your medicine. Should we ask Jack to help as well?"

Jack's head shot up at Raiden's words as we

stopped beside him. He looked like a kid with his hand caught in the cookie jar, and I couldn't figure out why. Raiden pulled my chair out for me, and as I sat down, I winced. Firestar chuckled and winked at me. I glared at him in return.

Our table consisted of my men and a few others I didn't recognize, one being a woman who was staring intently at me. She had pale hair like the others, but she kept hers braided with jewels and feathers threaded through them. Her eyes were a brilliant blue that reminded me of sapphires. She was absolutely beautiful despite the nasty look on her face. It was like she'd smelled something rancid, but when I sniffed myself, I didn't smell anything. Odd.

Either way, I was in too good of a mood to care. Still, one thing was definitely missing.

"So, where are Fujin and Raijin? Still in the infirmary?" I asked, turning to look at my men as I spoke.

"Yeah," Raiden said before picking up his silverware. "The lucky bastards have medics bringing them meals in bed. They even get to have sponge baths." He shook his head with a grin as he took a bite of his meal.

"I hardly think they would call themselves lucky." Firestar snorted. "Being beat to shit doesn't seem worth a few luxuries to me."

"You would if our lovely Maya were playing nurse." Raiden shot me a smoldering look that made me squirm in my seat. "What do you think Jack? Lucky or not?"

Jack who had been silent the entire time kept his eyes down on his plate as he muttered, "I don't have an opinion one way or another."

My brow furrowed at his answer. Something was off. I couldn't place my finger on it, but my dragon senses or rather my female senses were telling me something was going on. Something that my dear ol' Jack didn't want me to know about.

I picked up my glass and took a sip of it as I tried to decipher what had my mate in a mood. Then I remembered the woman at the table … or rather felt her. Her eyes hadn't moved from me since I sat down, and I could feel her gaze boring into my head as if she could shoot lasers out of her eyes.

"What's your problem?" I asked, turning my attention to the woman who instantly dropped her gaze. That didn't stop me any. "Well? You've been glaring at me ever since I arrived. Do you have a problem with me?"

"No," she said, her voice sultry and low. I wondered if that was her natural voice or if she did it on purpose. Bianca from Earth would have said she had a phone sex voice. The kind that made jealousy flare up inside of me.

"Maya." Jack placed his hand on my arm. My eyes went to that hand and then to his face. There was a nervousness there that made me pause.

"What?"

"Just ignore her," he answered, but when I waited for more, he just let the words hang in the air. That wasn't like him either.

I glanced at the woman as she stabbed her meal like it was her enemy before shifting my eyes back to Jack. Only my ice dragon kept his own gaze down as well. When Firestar and Raiden only shrugged in response to my inquiring eyes, I frowned. I couldn't figure out their connection. Why did she hate me so already and why would Jack jump to her defense, almost like...?

Then it clicked. An old lover.

"You know her, don't you?" I asked, turning back to Jack. "Who is she, Jack?"

"Nobody," he snapped, his eyes going to me with such irritation that I was taken back. When he saw my expression, the hard line of his lips softened. "I'm sorry. I didn't mean to snap. I mean, she doesn't matter."

"She sure seems like someone to me," I countered, my eyes going back to her. She was now staring at Jack as if he had ripped out her still-beating heart with his bare hands. "And that's not a look of someone who doesn't matter."

Jack sighed and leaned back from the table, slumping in his seat for the first time ever. "Gretchen. Her name is Gretchen, and we used to be lovers."

"Lovers?" Gretchen snarl-whispered. "That's all we were? Lovers? Or did you forget about the part where we were to be mated until your uncle sent you to her?!" She pointed her table knife at me with a vengeance. "Did you forget what you promised me?" She shook her knife with barely contained rage. "Is sharing her with *other men* really so good that you'd throw away everything we had?"

As Jack's eyes flitted between us, his mouth opened and closed like a dying fish, and with each moment that passed, my heart sank further into my feet. I'd felt the bitter sting of betrayal, and it had never hurt this much before. I reached into my boot and withdrew the dagger Jack had given me. I twisted it in my hands as I stared at the elegant blade. Taking a deep breath, I brought my eyes up and steadied them on Jack. "Did you lie to me?"

"Maya," Jack's voice broke, and that was all the answer I needed. When I'd found the dagger, I'd had this very thought. It had belonged to an old lover, someone he still held in his heart. When I had confronted him about it, he had told me the exact opposite, that he had meant it for me. Obviously, that was a lie as well.

I shoved my chair back, the feet of it scrapping the floor. Raiden and Firestar shifted as if to stand up but one look from me and they stayed seated. Jack stood as well, trying to get me to listen to him, but I was tired of hearing lies. I'd gotten myself into enough trouble with them that I didn't need any more burdening me.

"Don't." I pulled away from him, the tears wavering in my eyes making everything blur. "Don't stand there and lie to me again." I turned to Gretchen and threw the dagger on the table with a sad smile. "I suppose this belongs to you. I'm sorry for all the trouble I caused you."

Aware that the whole table was watching,

Gretchen didn't seem to let that bother her as stared at me as if I'd grown three heads and reached for the dagger, but Jack grabbed it before she could, causing her to growl. I didn't stay to find out what happened next, and my feet already carrying me out of the dining hall and down the corridor. The tears slipped free and slid down my face. I didn't bother to brush them away as I kept moving. I started to angle my path toward my bedroom but knew that would be the first place Jack would look for me. I didn't want to see him or anyone right now.

Funny how a few minutes could completely change your wants. Just before that, I had wanted nothing more than to curl up with my men and bask in their presence. Now, I wished I was back on Earth, eating bad food with Ryan, making fun of insta-love movies where the couple always ended with a happily ever after.

But real life wasn't like that. It was cold and ruthless. It didn't care if you were happy before. That gave it all the more reason to bitch slap you with reality.

I shoved through the main doors and into the cold air, but I barely felt it against my hot cheeks. I trudged down the hay-covered path, my arms wrapped around myself as if they would keep the hurt inside me from bursting out. A few people hung around outside, their curious gazes watching me as I passed by. I ignored them, not caring what anyone thought of me. It wasn't like they knew who I was.

The smell of roasted nuts hit my nose and the nausea I had been able to hold back all day hit me full force. I had a split second to rush off the path before my stomach emptied itself beside a merchant's booth. A warm hand patted my back as the heaves subsided, and I dared to look back.

"Are you, all right?" the old man from the first day asked me.

Flushing with embarrassment, I nodded. "Yeah, just one of the many pleasures of being pregnant." I gave a bitter chuckle.

The man gave me a sympathetic look before scooping up some snow from the ground. "Here, for your mouth."

I looked at it curiously and then accepted it, taking some into my mouth before spitting it out and using the rest to wipe off my face. When I was clean, and my mouth didn't taste like a dead rat, I turned to the man. "Thank you."

"No trouble at all." The old man smiled. "I'm

Marcus. Why don't you come to my home and warm up? You shouldn't be out here without a coat in your condition."

I rubbed my arms and nodded gratefully for the offer. At least I won't run into anyone I knew at his home.

Marcus led me away from the center square and to a modestly sized home.

"My late wife and I built this home ourselves right after we were married," Marcus explained, quite proud of himself. As he should be.

"It's lovely."

He nodded his head and reached for something on the shelf next to him and handed it to me. "We had five children."

I glanced down at the picture he had handed me, the large group of smiling faces made my jaw drop.

Marcus laughed at my gaping mouth. "I know quite a lot for most dragons, but my lovely bride always wanted a big family and, so she had it."

"Do you get to see them often?" I asked as we sat down before the fire in his home. The inside reflected the man across from me, worn but well loved. I hoped one day to have someone come into my home and think the same thing.

"Not a lot," he said, sadness on his face, but then he smiled. "But they will all be here to celebrate the winter's games. I look forward to it every year."

"Yes, I hear it's a lot of fun," I commented with a nod as I rubbed my hands and pointed them toward the fire. I could feel my toes again finally.

"Are you going to participate?" Marcus asked curiously. "Many women do, even in your condition."

I frowned and shook my head. "No, my ..." I hesitated not sure how to explain my relationship with all three men but then decided to just be honest. "My mates are pretty overprotective. They don't want me to get hurt."

"Mates huh?" Marcus smiled a twinkled of mischief in his eyes. "You are lucky to have so many who love you, especially with our dear Jack as your companion."

The mention of Jack caused a pang of pain in my chest. I gave him a small smile, trying my best not to reveal how tormented I felt. "Yes, I'm very lucky."

"And a child as well. The gods must be looking down on you. Too many dragonesses live their whole life without ever knowing the love of a child."

I laughed. "If I am blessed by the gods, you must be a favorite. Five children and even more grandchildren." I raised a brow, and we smiled together.

"Yes, I suppose I am," Marcus murmured to himself, his eyes going to the fire. After a moment, he opened his mouth to tell me something else but then stopped, his attention going to the door. Not a second later, someone pounded on it.

Standing from his seat, he made his way to the door. He opened it slightly, but I couldn't see who it was from my spot by the fire. There was a soft exchange of words before Marcus led whoever it was into the house.

Firestar. My eyes widened when I saw the large man, and then my gaze fell onto my lap. Just seeing him reminded me of my pain.

"Maya," Firestar started, kneeling at my feet. "We've been looking everywhere for you."

"I know. I'm sorry." I lowered my head further, knowing I shouldn't have left alone. We'd just had a discussion about my safety, and here I was making rash decisions once more.

"It's all right." Firestar smoothed his hand down my back and then urged me to my feet. "Let's just get you home and to bed. Are you hungry? I can have food brought to your room."

I shook my head. "No, I'm fine." I let Firestar lead me to the front door, but stopped so I could thank Marcus. "I really appreciate your hospitality."

"You are always welcome in this home," the older man replied with a genuine grin. "Now, you take care of those men of yours and don't let them smother you too much. A dragoness needs to be free to fly, or she will die." This time his words were directed at Firestar who only huffed in response.

We were silent on our way back to the house. Firestar thankfully didn't pry, and I could keep my emotions bundled up where they belonged. At least for now.

When he brought me back to my room, I held onto his sleeve, not letting him leave me. "Please, just stay with me tonight." My lip wavered as I asked, and I knew my time of being brave was almost over.

Firestar inclined his head and opened the bedroom door just as Jack came out of his. His pale eyes landed on me, and I had to duck behind Firestar to keep him from coming up to me.

"Maya," Jack pleaded, his voice full of distress. "Please let me explain."

"Not tonight," Firestar snapped, his hand coming up to stop Jack from getting to me.

"Get out of my way," Jack growled in return, something I'd rarely heard him do.

His threat was wasted on Firestar. The fire dragon shook his head and shoved Jack back a step. "She's been through enough today. If she wants to talk to you, she will, but either way, it's not happening tonight." This time his tone left no room for argument as he ushered me into my bedroom, slamming the door shut before locking it for good measure.

"Thank you," I breathed when we were finally alone.

"Don't worry about it."

He didn't say anything more as I dressed for bed. After Firestar did the same, we climbed into bed, and he pulled me to him so that I was curled into his front. That was when the tears started. Unlike before, these weren't silent tears but wracking sobs that I would definitely be embarrassed about later but right now, I couldn't care less.

Firestar rubbed my back, making shushing noises as he rocked me. He didn't try to talk to me or ask me to explain, something I was grateful for. He was simply there.

It ironic that my one mate was comforting me about my other mate. It really wasn't a situation I would have ever thought I'd be in. I made a choking laugh that had Firestar's hand pausing mid rub.

"What is it?" he asked, glancing down at me.

Eyes pricking with tears, I gave him a watery smile. "I was just thinking how messed up we are. You comforting me because my other boyfriend made me cry."

Firestar snorted. "Not messed up at all. Even if we weren't mated, I would still be here for you."

"To get in my pants you mean."

He shook his head with a serious look on his face. "No. While I do enjoy every part of your delectable little body, I would never take advantage of you while you were hurting." Firestar stroked a thumb over my cheek catching the moisture that had fallen. "I've loved you since before all this, and I will love you still even if you end up only wanting one of us."

I shook my head, unable to hide my smile. "Never going to happen. You're a part of me now, you couldn't get rid of me even if you tried." I brushed my lips across his and then sank back into his embrace, my heart not hurting quite as much as before.

Even if Jack was an inconsiderate asshole at least I had Firestar and Raiden to keep me from completely falling apart. With that thought, my eyes grew heavy, tired of all the drama but before I could drift off to sleep, a knock came to the door.

I glanced up at Firestar who answered, "Who is it?"

"It's me," Raiden's voice came through the other side.

Firestar glanced down at me, and I nodded my consent to let him in. Sliding from the bed, he unlocked the door but only opened it slightly, making sure it was really him. When satisfied, he moved aside to let Raiden in before closing and locking the door again.

"Hey, love." Raiden came over to the other side of the bed. Firestar crawled back into his spot, pulling me back into his arms.

"I don't want to talk about it," was all I could croak out before burying my face back into Firestar's chest.

"That's all right." Raiden's side of the bed shifted, and his body lined up along the back of mine. "I'm just going to be here if you need me. No talking required."

I sighed and leaned into him. The feeling of being surrounded should have made me feel claustrophobic, but at that moment I only felt protected. Too bad that with all their muscle, they couldn't protect a broken heart.

10

What could be the worst thing to happen after you get your heart broken? Waking up alone.

I fell asleep snuggled in two of my mates' arms and woke up to empty bed sheets with neither of them anywhere to be found. I had an urge to just bury myself back into the bed and wallow in my misery, but something inside of me said no.

I wasn't going to be that woman who let a man destroy her. I still had Raiden and Firestar, even if Jack ended up being a lying asshole. Besides, I had a child to worry about. I couldn't let my misery affect him or her.

Jumping out of bed, I headed for the shower

but froze in my steps. "What if it's Jack's?" I whispered to myself, stunned by the prospect.

I half laughed, half cried, and almost crumbled in the middle of the room as I became overwhelmed by emotion. All this time, I'd been trying to get pregnant and worried about whose baby it was, terrified even. If it was Jack's, I didn't want that reminder of his lies day in and day out. And what if he wanted to be in the child's life? That would mean he'd still have to be in my life and with *her*.

Hold on a second, I'm getting ahead of myself.

I still hadn't heard Jack's explanation. He was with me after all and had said he loved me. Could I so easily toss him aside without hearing his side of the story?

Yes, one side of me hissed, while the other side cried out a resounding no. With my mind at war, it was obvious what I had to do. I needed to get the whole story before passing judgment. I might be hormonal, but I wasn't an idiot. Losing one of the men I loved because I jumped to the wrong conclusions wasn't something I wanted to tell my child, especially, if Jack ended up being the father.

Sighing, I jerked my hand through my hair, wincing as they caught on a handful of tangles.

First, a shower. I glanced at the clock by the bed and saw it was barely seven o'clock. Forget a shower, I wanted a nice relaxing bath. Hopefully, after that, I would be ready for whatever it was Jack had to say.

An hour later, I was clean and dry, but no readier to face the day than I had been before. I dug through the magic bag the twins had given us, searching for the clothes they had provided. My hands touched something soft, so soft that I pulled it out of the bag without hesitation.

That something ended up being a dress. Dyed a pale green, it had long sleeves and a low neckline. It was a dress meant to seduce and enamor. It really wasn't something one should wear to a meeting of hearts, but since I felt like crap, I might as well look good. If it made Jack suffer, all the better.

Slipping into the dress, I let out a low purr. The dress felt even better on me than in my hand, and it hugged my body perfectly. I found the mirror and twirled a bit, smiling as the skirt swirled around my legs. Dresses weren't really my thing, but everyone deserved to feel pretty every once in a while. I needed that now more than ever.

After plaiting my hair, I headed for the door. My hand on the doorknob, I hesitated. There were voices in the hallway. My tongue seemed to swell, making my mouth feel dry and unusable. I wasn't ready for this. I didn't want to hear Jack tell me he never loved me, that it was all a lie. I'd rather pretend like I already knew and ignore it all. Leave even.

But I knew I couldn't. There wasn't anywhere else for me to go. If I went back home, Ned might kill me. If I went east, Lady Nariko would definitely kill me or worse breed me. Firestar's father wasn't trustworthy, even with the promise of gold. God knew what the unaligned would do to me and finding a portal to Earth was nearly impossible.

No, I had to do this. I couldn't hide in my room wondering what Jack might say. Better to get it over with quickly, and then rip the bastard's throat out with my teeth.

Taking a deep breath, I turned the knob and entered the hallway. Right outside, my eyes found Jack with Firestar and Raiden. They were talking in low voices, but not so much that I couldn't hear them from the room.

"You need to tread carefully," Firestar warned. "She's very fragile right now, and I won't let your fuck-up cause her more pain."

"I don't wish to cause her pain at all," Jack

growled in return. He had bags under his eyes, and his clothes were wrinkled as if he had slept in them. Good to know I wasn't the only one who suffered, a petty side of me thought.

"Still," Raiden interjected, "you need to be clear with her. Don't lie, don't try to do that political side-stepping bullshit you do. Tell her the truth. The whole truth and pray to the gods she forgives your sorry ass."

My lips ticked up as Raiden reamed Jack. At least, they had my back. Still, the moment Jack's eyes flickered up to find mine, my face fell. My feet moved backward on their own, and I was half tempted to run, but I forced them to stop. No more running. I could do this.

"Maya," Jack breathed, causing Raiden and Firestar to turn. Their eyes landed on my face, and there was an array of emotions on display there. Firestar seemed angry, while Raiden only seemed sad. I didn't know who their emotions were targeted toward and didn't really care to ask. My heart was in my throat, and I could feel the bile threatening to rise.

Raiden approached me first, his hand going to my face. "Give him a chance to explain. We'll be here for you, no matter what you decide."

I swallowed thickly and nodded once. Firestar didn't say anything. Instead, he kissed me on the forehead before he and Raiden started down the hallway, leaving Jack and me alone.

We stayed on our sides of the hallway, neither of us speaking at first. I didn't want to be the one who broke the silence. It wasn't me who screwed up, but I also wasn't going to stand there all day.

"You wanted to speak to me?" I cleared my throat as I stiffened my spine.

"Yes," Jack answered, taking a step toward me. I forced myself not to take a step back, reminding myself that this was Jack. No matter what he may have lied about, he wouldn't hurt me.

Tell that to my heart.

"Let's not do this here," Jack continued, his gaze moving around the hallway.

"What? Afraid of being overhead and having your precious reputation tarnished?" I sneered, knowing I was being nasty.

Pressing his lips tightly together, Jack nodded. "I deserve that and much more, but I ask for privacy for your sake, not mine."

He was right. I didn't want to do this with an audience, not with how easy it had been for me to cry. Breaking down in the privacy of your own room was one thing. Doing it in the middle of the hallway was another.

"Fine." I sniffed and turned toward my bedroom. "Better to hide a body in any case."

Jack didn't respond to my thinly veiled threat. Not that I'd act on it. While my heart did ache, I had a hard time believing I could ever do anything to him, no matter how much I wanted to.

With the door shut firmly behind us, I stood by the bed as far away from him as I could get. Jack tried to come closer, but I held up a hand, shaking my head. "No, I said I'd listen to you. That doesn't mean I want you near me."

Sighing but giving in to my request, Jack leaned against the opposite wall. "First off, let me tell you how sorry I am that you had to find out that way. I had hoped Gretchen wouldn't show up, but she had somehow gotten wind that I was back."

"Of course, she did." I sneered. "Her lost love was back. If I were in her place, I'd be thinking all sorts of things. And I'm sure you did everything in your power to make sure she knew her place, didn't you?"

"Not exactly," Jack admitted with a frown. "I didn't have time. She kind of ambushed me at dinner and then you showed up." He gave a bitter chuckle. "It was a bit of a surprise for both of you, believe me."

I did actually. The look on Gretchen's face when I had arrived had been confused and curious at first. Of course, she figured out quickly who I was, and that Jack hadn't come back to her. I could just imagine the rage that coursed through her. Probably a bit like mine now.

"So, what about the dagger?" I asked, trying to be civil and not bite his head off. "Why not just tell me the truth?"

"Because," - Jack let out a heavy breath - "I didn't want you to doubt my affections after we had just overcome such a big hurdle."

"I'd have understood, though," I argued. "I didn't expect you all to come to me chaste. I didn't expect anything of you at all. Yet, you let me believe I was the only one who had your heart."

"You do!" Jack pushed off the wall and came toward me. "I cared for Gretchen deeply, and yes, we were to be officially mated, but after I met you, after I really got to know you, I realized I didn't know love until you."

He grabbed my hands as he knelt in front of me. I wanted to pull away, but I couldn't find the strength. "You sparked something in me that no one else ever has. Gretchen will always have a place in my heart, but you have the rest of it. Don't tell me you can't understand."

The problem was I could. I could understand. I fell in love with Firestar and adding him to my little harem of men had been so easy. I'd thought I'd lost all the love I had for him, but just seeing him rekindled some of that love, giving him the opportunity to win me back. There was only one question though.

"Do you still love her?" I asked, my voice low and fragile as if I'd break at any moment. "Do you want to stay here ... with her?"

"No, no," Jack answered, shaking his head as he pulled me into his arms. I let him hold me as he kissed my forehead. "Even if we didn't start off on the best footing, I chose you. I could have let Raiden have you and come back at any time, but I didn't."

That he was right about. He could have left me at any time, and let Raiden be the winner. He had, after all, gotten to me first. But the fact that Jack hadn't left said something profound, something that meant he really was telling the truth this time.

"I believe you," I murmured into his ear, holding him close to me.

Jack held me tighter, his face buried in my neck. He pulled away slightly to press his lips to mine in a desperate kiss. I kissed him back with just as much ferocity. A possessive part of me wanted to remind him who he belonged to, and I flipped him on his back, pinning his hands above his head. I knew he could get away at any moment, but the fact that he didn't leave told me told me more than any words could have that he wanted to be here. With me.

"Tell me you love me," I commanded, bending down to nip at his lower lip.

"I love you."

"Tell me you want me," I demanded, again biting at him. I felt something hard stir beneath me and knew before he said it what the answer was.

"Oh, I'll always want you."

Jack pressed his hips against mine to prove the point. I rocked my center against him, letting out a deep gurgling moan, but when Jack tried to flip us, I jumped up from the bed. I smirked at the look of confusion on his face.

"Not yet. I might believe you," I swayed slightly back and forth letting the full effect of the dress settle on him, "but that doesn't mean I forgive you, not just yet." I gave him a coy grin before starting for the door. Jack caught up with me, his arms wrapping around my waist as he pinned me there.

Nipping at my exposed shoulder, Jack stroked my stomach. "I will do whatever it takes to get back into your good graces, my love."

"Anything?" I asked with a raised brow even though he couldn't see it.

"Yes. Just name it." His hand stroked downward to caress me through my dress. I closed my eyes for a moment, giving into his touch before pushing his hand away.

"I'm sure I will think of something." I opened the door and trotted down the hallway with Jack close on my heels. Being in charge for once was good.

11

———

The games started today. After my little melodrama, I needed something to distract me. Too bad the center of that drama didn't go away.

"Jack," Gretchen purred, blatantly ignoring me. "I had hoped you would show up. Are you going to participate in the games?"

"As always," Jack stiffly replied, much to my delight. His cold response was the only thing keeping me from ripping the woman's face off.

Gretchen didn't seem to notice his lack of interest. She ran her hand up and down Jack's chest, pushing her own out so that most of her breasts were proudly displayed above her shirt. "Well, let me be the first to give you a good luck kiss."

"No, thanks. I have all the luck I need right here." Jack quickly disentangled himself from her roaming hands and pulled me to his side. I wrapped my arms around him a victorious grin on my face.

Now forced to admit I existed, Gretchen's face twisted into a snarl. "Any bitch who has to have more than one man doesn't deserve someone like Jack," she spat in my face.

Flicking a finger across my cheek where her spittle had landed, I took a step forward. "At least I know when I'm not wanted. Unlike you."

Gretchen opened her mouth to say something more, but Jack stepped between us. "I think that's about enough of that. Come, Maya. The others are waiting." Jack shot Gretchen a warning look before directing me over to where Raiden and Firestar stood with a group of others.

When we approached, my men turned to greet us. Firestar didn't seem surprised, while Raiden just looked happy it was all over.

"They say there's a man here who has been the winner every year, and no one has beaten him." Raiden rubbed his hands together in excitement, clearly ignoring what had just happened.

"How an undefeated opponent excites you, I have no idea," I said, shrugging.

"That sound challenging," Firestar drew out as he rubbed his chin before turning to Jack. "Tell us what you know about this unbeaten warrior."

"Well," Jack began with a hint of a grin on his lips, "I hear he's quick and smart. A great dresser." He adjusted his sleeves with a sniff. "And handsome to boot."

I shoved at him with a laugh. "Jack, you're the champion, aren't you?"

Jack's smile broadened, and he straightened his back. "Well, I wouldn't say champion but a winner, yes."

"Good." Firestar nodded, an excited gleam in his eye. "We will finally get to see what we are all made of."

"Uh-uh." I held a hand up before they could start berating each other more. "Do you want what happened back at Raiden's to happen here?" The guys just looked at me like I was stupid. "You showed your powers to Raiden's brothers, his mother saw, and she tried to whore me out, Remember?" Irritation colored my words at having to remind them. It was quite a traumatic event. I didn't like thinking about it myself.

"Oh, yes. I do believe you are right." Jack frowned. "It would probably be best to keep our extra abilities," he used air quotes around the word before continuing, "to ourselves. Only use them in dire need."

"We're talking life or death here." I gestured at Raiden and especially Firestar, the most likely of the three to show off.

Raiden held his hands up with a grin. "Don't look at me. I'm not the one with an over-inflated ego."

"And I am?" Firestar snarled, grabbing Raiden by the collar. "I could pound you into the ground where you stand."

"See?" Raiden pointed a finger at Firestar, looking at Jack and me. "Can't even take criticism."

"Knock it off, you two." Jack shook his head, disappointment clear in his voice. "We have bigger problems to worry about, like what we discussed." They exchanged a look that I didn't understand.

"What?" My eyes went to each of them. "What did you discuss?"

Firestar sighed, clearly not happy with whatever it was. "We decided that you should be able to participate in the games."

"Really?" My eyes widened, a giddy grin covering my lips. "I can really compete?" My grin fell as I pointed a suspicious finger at them. "What about not getting hurt?"

"That's where the catch is," Raiden answered. "You can compete, but only in the hunt. And," he held up a hand before I could answer, "only if one of us comes with you."

Clapping my mouth shut, I thought about his offer. I wanted to compete, true, but not with so many stipulations. I really should have quit while I was ahead, but I couldn't help myself.

"Why can't I race? Flying isn't going to get me killed."

Firestar snorted. "Says the woman who still gets tired after an hour of leisure flying. A race would be far too dangerous at your flying level."

"No, it wouldn't," I argued back.

Jack placed a hand on my arm and shook his head. "This race is for advanced fliers. Only masters are allowed to enter. Since you are a late bloomer, you wouldn't be allowed to compete, anyway."

"Fine." I sighed in defeat. I couldn't really argue with rules. Besides, the idea of flying against a bunch of unknown people didn't sit well. I didn't want to get knocked out of the sky.

"Good, it's settled." Firestar turned to leave, but I stopped him.

"Not so fast. Why do I need a chaperone on the hunt? It's not really fair if we are working together. What will the others say?" I glanced at them, hoping to prod at their sense of honor.

This time Raiden stepped in. "It's not up for discussion. Either you go with one of us or not at all. We can't risk someone attacking you when you are out there on your own."

Crossing my arms over my chest, I pouted. "Fine. I guess I can live with that."

"Good. Now, stop your pouting and come cheer me on." Firestar smirked as he headed toward the fighting ring.

"Cheer you on?" Raiden called after him. "I'm afraid you will be waiting a while for that because she'll be cheering me on." Raiden shot me a grin and a wink as he chased after Firestar.

"Children, the lot of them." Jack offered me a smile and his arm. "They should know by now that it is *I* you will be rooting for."

"Is that so?" I raised a brow. "Maybe I won't cheer for any of you. Maybe I'll find another to scream for."

Jack leaned down to my ear and said in a low

voice, "Oh, you will scream all right, but it will only be my name falling from your lips."

I shivered at his words as they shot straight through me and into my aching core. I had been the one to start this game, but Jack seemed determined to finish it. There was a part of me that couldn't wait to see him try.

We all gathered around the ring the villagers had set up. Plenty of them were placing bets on who they thought might win. I stood next to Raiden and Jack as we watched Firestar get ready for his fight. His opponent was half his size, but you wouldn't know it from the way he snarled and hopped around like he was the shit.

"They call him Buzzard," Jack said from my side, leaning against the pole of the ring. His eyes were firmly on the male across from Firestar. "He might not look like much, but he's quick and can be pretty vicious. Firestar will be flat on his ass if he doesn't knock him out fast."

"He's that good?" I asked, leaning forward to get a better look at the pipsqueak. Buzzard, huh? He had a pointed face, and a buzzed haircut. I didn't have to think hard about why exactly he had gained the nickname.

"Not really." Jack sniffed. "He's just sneaky."

"Well, one thing's for sure," Raiden said with a cheeky grin. "This is going to be one hell of a fight."

The crowd cheered, dragging our attention back to the two in the ring. Lord Fafnir stood near the two, a pleased expression on his face. He waited for the crowd to calm down before speaking.

"Thank you, thank you all for coming to this season's games!" At Lord Fafnir's words, the crowd roared so loud the ground shook. "We have some great competitors this year, starting with our very own Buzzard." Lord Fafnir waited while the crowd went wild, hushing them with a wave of his hands. "And fighting against him is one of the fiery dragons of the south, Firestar!"

There were a few boos and jeers, but the guys and I tried to overpower them with our own shouts. A few of the dragons shot dirty looks our way, and I had the urge to flip them off before I decided against it. No starting fights outside the ring. I'm going to be a mother now. Fighting should be the last thing on my mind.

Before I knew it, the fight had started. I ripped myself away from my thoughts to make sure I didn't miss a thing.

Firestar didn't wait for Buzzard to attack him first. The fire dragon darted forward, fist lashing out as a terrifying growl exploded from his lips.

Buzzard dodged, using his smaller size to his advantage. As he nimbly slid past Firestar's blow, his leg shot out, catching Firestar right in the gut.

Air whooshed from Firestar's mouth as he grabbed his stomach, doubling over as the crowd went crazy. Buzzard slammed his elbow down on Firestar's back, knocking him to the ground.

"That's it, crawl on the ground like the disgusting worm you are," Buzzard cried, dancing from foot to foot and throwing a few punches at the air as Firestar collapsed.

Only, instead of taking a face full of dirt, Firestar hit the ground in a roll, coming up to his feet behind Buzzard.

The smaller dragon tried to whirl around, but Firestar stepped in, kicking the back of Buzzard's knee, knocking him off balance. As Buzzard's hands went out in a futile effort to regain his balance, Firestar wrapped an arm around Buzzard's neck, cutting off his air supply.

Buzzard struggled, trying to reach up and pry Firestar's arm away even as the fire dragon shifted his stance, driving his hip into Buzzard and lifting the man off his feet so that his own bodyweight increased the pressure on his throat.

Buzzard's eyes bugged out of his head as he began slapping frantically behind himself, desperate to injure Firestar, but since he couldn't get the leverage he needed to do any lasting harm.

"Yield," Firestar said as the little man's blows weakened, but even still, he didn't concede.

As his body went limp, Firestar released Buzzard, dropping him to the ground.

"Looks like we have a winner." Lord Fafnir clapped a hand on Firestar's arm as a medic rushed into the ring to check on Buzzard.

Boos filled the stands as Firestar stood there, clearly pleased with himself.

"Looks like I'm not making any friends here," Firestar scoffed as he climbed out of the ring. He clapped Raiden on the arm. "You're up."

Raiden turned to me, taking my hand in his. "Very well, I will show our pretty lady exactly how it is done." He pressed his lips to the back of my hand, sending a shiver down my spine.

Firestar snorted. "We'll see who's laughing when you get knocked on your ass."

"That will never happen," Raiden smirked as he climbed into the ring.

I bit my lip and smiled as I watched him walk away. My grin quickly fell when I realized who his opponent was.

Gretchen.

"Don't worry," Jack said, clearly reading the distress on my face. "Raiden will be fine."

"I wasn't worried about him." I glared up at Jack before turning my eyes back to the fight. I had a sudden urge to put on a cheerleading outfit and start doing cartwheels, anything if it meant knocking that smug bitch on her ass.

The guys had agreed not to use their powers I'd given them. We couldn't have too many people looking our way. Besides, it would give them an unfair advantage. So, Raiden was going to have to beat Gretchen the old fashion way, and if the shit-eating grin on his face meant anything, he was going to enjoy every moment of it.

Once again, the crowd was on the ice dragon's side, not that it bothered Raiden much. He shuffled his feet and lifted his hands up, curling them into fists. Ready, he shot Gretchen one of his panty-melting grins. I'd have been upset had I not known he planned to beat the crap out of her.

Gretchen seemed taken back by Raiden's expression but shook it off. She held her hands out to her sides, her fingers glowing blue as her magic awakened. That couldn't be good.

"Raiden, don't let her touch you!" I shouted over the bar of the ring.

Raiden shot a look to Gretchen's hand, his smile wilting slightly, but then he was back to his usual self. Lord Fafnir approached, and everyone waited for him to make his announcement, the anticipation thick in the air.

"From the East, we have Raiden, third son of Lord Shen!" Lord Fafnir gestured toward Raiden who smiled and waved, shooting a wink and an air kiss my way. The crowd was a bit more receiving of him than Firestar, probably all his flirting from before.

"Fighting against him is our very own ball busting sweetheart, Gretchen!" The crowd loved Gretchen, they screamed and cheered some even shouted mating proposals to her. Just hearing Lord Fafnir talk about her that way, made my heart clench tight. If the crowd had their way, Jack would have been with Gretchen and not me.

Suddenly, a jealous sadistic side of me wanted

Raiden to make the bitch bleed. I shook the visual out of my head as Lord Fafnir moved to a safe distance. It was about to start.

As soon as the bell rang, Gretchen lunged forward, icy-blue hands streaking through the air in a blur of frosty energy.

Raiden sidestepped as sparks began to dance along his flesh. His palm darted out, catching her in the side and knocking her off balance right before a bolt of lightning leapt from his outstretched fingers.

Electricity surged across her skin, causing her muscles to seize and spasm. Unable to catch her balance, she crashed to the floor in a spray of dirt. Steam curled off of her as she lay there for a moment.

"What are you doing? Finish her off," I cried as Raiden took a quick step backward, trying to put some distance between them.

"He can't," Jack said, whispering in my ear as his hand darted out to point. That's when I realized that frost had spread out along the ground where Gretchen lay. "If he touches that, he risks getting himself frozen."

"Damn, stalling bitch," I grumbled as Raiden raised one hand to the sky. Overhead lightning cracked across the sky, and I realized he was about to bring the thunder.

"I'd wanted to make this quick," Gretchen said as she pushed herself to her feet. "But, I guess that's not in the cards now." A small smile curled across her lips. "Too bad."

As she raised one perfectly manicured hand and pointed at him, frost exploded from the group, ripping toward him in an avalanche of icicles that gleamed in the light.

Raiden dove to the left, the lightning he'd been calling dissipating in an instant as he rolled across the ground. The wave smashed into the railing behind where he'd stood a moment later, fast-freezing the wall and sheathing the ground in slick ice.

Worse, as Raiden came to his feet, Gretchen was already there. Her nails grew longer into claws as she swiped at him. He jumped out of the way fast enough to save his skin but not his shirt. Her claws gouged through the fabric, rending it to pieces as he called on his lightning.

"Hey! This is my favorite shirt," Raiden snapped as he flung the bolt of lightning at her.

"Funny. I think it'd look better in the trash,"

Gretchen replied, dodging lithely by his lightning before stomping on the ground.

Spears of ice exploded from beneath Raiden's feet as he sprang skyward. His wings burst from his back, holding him in the air as the entire arena became a deathtrap of razor-sharp icicles.

"That won't be enough to stop me," Raiden said, and as he spoke the sky above crackled angrily. "You'd best give up now."

"Oh?" she arched an eyebrow at him, and as she spoke, blue energy exploded out from her feet, fast freezing the ground of the entire arena. Frost crawled over the railing, turning the benches into crystal as the spectators' benches became sheathed in ice. "Would you really shoot me?"

"Spiteful bitch, isn't she?" Firestar growled, shooting a glare at Jack.

Jack pressed his lips into a thin line. "Yes, she can have a temper."

I couldn't disagree with him there.

Gretchen was a smart one though, I had to give her that. As I stared down at the frost beneath my feet, I wanted to curse. By icing over the entire area, she limited Raiden's lightning powers. If he wanted to hit her with a bolt, he had to be willing to zap the whole crowd, including me, which he wouldn't do.

I hoped.

Raiden eyed the ice with a frown on his face, while Gretchen stayed on the ground. Worse, it made sense. Raiden was a lightning dragon, and aerial combat was one of his specialties. Only now, he wouldn't be able to use that to his advantage. No. He'd have to come down and fight her on the ground, and what's more, he'd be limited in what he could do.

"See, here's the thing," Raiden said. "Wait, what's that?" Raiden screwed up his face in confusion and pointed right at me. "Maya, don't!"

Gretchen turned, her gaze flicking to me, and as she did, Raiden darted forward. His fist arched through the air, and as Gretchen realized her mistake and turned back toward him, his fist caught her in the chin, sending her spinning like a top. She crashed through part of the ice, shattering it beneath the force of the blow.

Gretchen cried out in pain, one hand outstretched as a huge slab of ice erupted from the ground between them, shielding her before he could continue the onslaught. Only, she needn't have bothered because Raiden didn't press the attack. Instead, he darted across the ring, hitting the corner before springing off into the next.

"What the hell is he doing?" Firestar gaped, shaking his head in confusion. "This isn't a dance competition; it's a fight."

"He's not playing," Jack announced. Firestar and I turned to him and found Jack nodding toward the ring with a hint of amusement on his lips. "Just watch. Our boy is smarter than you give him credit for, Firestar."

Turning my eyes back to the fight, I watched Raiden for some hidden meaning in his movements. I still didn't see it though. It just looked like he was dancing around the ring sporadically. One good thing was that Gretchen seemed to be in the dark as well.

She'd recovered from his attack and stood there, clearly annoyed. "What the hell are you doing?" she snapped, glaring at him as blue energy began to swirl around her.

At the sound of her voice, Raiden stopped. He eyed his work with a grin. "Oh, you'll see." Raiden raised his hand toward the air, and it crackled with power.

"He's going to hit the lot of us!" a male ice dragon near us cried out, causing a commotion in the crowd as people began to search for cover.

Eyes wide, I turned to Jack who didn't seem as

concerned as he should have been. In fact, he was laughing.

"What's so funny?" I shoved a hand at him causing him to choke on his chuckle. "He's going to hit us with that or did you forget?"

Jack shook his head and placed a hand on my shoulder, turning me back to the fight. "No, he won't. Just watch."

While the dragons around us fought to get away from the ring, we and surprisingly Lord Fafnir stayed behind. He must have realized whatever it was Jack had as well. I just wished the guys had let me in on it.

"You aren't going to do it," Gretchen taunted, her hands on her hips with a sneer. "You hit me, and your precious mate will get hit too." She spat the word in my direction. I'd have been offended if I didn't think she was about to get zapped.

"Oh, I wouldn't be so sure about that." Raiden shot me a wink before he took the handful of lightning and slammed it into the ground.

Lightning swept through the ice, electrifying the ground. Gretchen couldn't get away fast enough. Electricity surged through her, sending her body into spasms that shook her body so hard she couldn't even scream.

While I watched her vibrate, I braced myself for a shock of a lifetime, but it never came. The lightning didn't even come close to anyone outside the ring. That's when I saw it.

The rivets in the ice.

"That's how he did it!" I cried out, pointing at the ground. "He wasn't dancing. He was splitting the ice so his lightning wouldn't be conducted to us."

"He's either smarter than I thought or even more of an idiot." Firestar grinned, too proud to admit he was impressed.

As Gretchen collapsed to the ground, still convulsing, Lord Fafnir stood and nodded, a smile on his face.

"Well played, Raiden." He gestured at the lightning dragon. "It seems you've won this round."

Raiden did a little bow which was received with a mixed response. No one really knew what to think. He had outsmarted all of us, that was for sure.

"Well, while this has been educational," Firestar cleared his throat before nodding to Jack as Raiden approached us. "You're up, buddy."

"It would seem so. I'll try to put on a show for you that rivals even Raiden's." Jack's pale blue gaze met mine, and I reached out and ran my hand through his long white hair with a smile.

"Go kick some ass."

12

The crowd shifted, and excitement filled the air. It was as if they knew who would fight next and they couldn't wait.

I knew I couldn't.

"Are you ready?" I asked Jack as he took in the crowd.

He didn't seem worried at all. "Of course. I prepared all year for this, why wouldn't I be?" Jack shot me a breathtaking smile before climbing into the ring.

The crowd roared when they saw him. He was an obvious favorite of the village. Not that I could blame him, he was one of mine too.

The poor bastard fighting him didn't get much

of a reaction, sadly. I almost felt bad for him being outcheered by my guy, though, not as bad as he was going to feel when Jack knocked him out.

Moderately built and shoulder length hair, I didn't pay enough attention to catch his name but knew he wouldn't last long. There was a bit of a quaking to his movements as if he was a half-second away from running for the hills.

When Lord Fafnir called the fight to start, the man did indeed run. Around the ring that is. He darted back forward, never staying still long enough for Jack to get a hit in which was probably the point.

With each swing, Jack grew more impatient. His demeanor changed as the smile slipped off his face, and he lashed out, fist arching through the air to once again catch a whole lot of nothing.

"Stop running," Jack said, voice cold and angry. "It's no fun for anyone."

"Don't be mad because you're too slow," his competitor called, then he stuck his tongue out. "That's it!" Jack sprinted forward, tearing across the ring, and as he did, I caught a flash of a grin on his opponent's face.

"Jack, watch out!" I cried just as his no-name

opponent struck. He shifted forward on his heels as his left foot shot out in a kick that would have leveled Jack.

As it stood, Jack barely had time to dodge. He stepped sideways, feet sliding across the ring as his opponent's foot whipped by him.

Unfortunately, the guy hadn't counted on missing, and as he stumbled forward off balance, Jack slammed his elbow into his back of his head.

The speedy fighter crashed to the ground, and as he lay there, I realized he was out cold.

"That was quick." Lord Fafnir eased into the ring and pushed Jack's foe with the edge of his boot. He grunted but didn't get up.

With a disappointed huff, Lord Fafnir turned to Jack. "Looks like we have a winner!"

The crowd clapped and cheered, but overall, they seemed as disappointed as Lord Fafnir was. Apparently, that was too easy of a win for their precious Jack.

"Good job." I smiled at Jack as he came back to our side.

Jack scoffed. "Hardly a decent fight. I'd expected more."

"Yeah, that guy was a bit lacking, that's for

sure." Raiden shook his head, clearly unhappy with the fight.

"So, what's next?" Firestar asked.

"We eat lunch, and then the next round begins." Jack offered me his arm, which I gladly took.

As we made our way back to the main house, several dragons clapped Jack on the back and either congratulated him or expressing their disappointment. If the next rounds didn't sate the crowd, we might have a riot on our hands.

"What will the next round be like?" I asked as we took our seats in the dining hall. "Will you guys go against one another?"

"The next round," Jack started as he filled his plate with various meats, cheeses, and nuts, "we'll face off with the winner of the other rounds until there are only two left. Then those two will fight until there is but one."

Raiden shoved food into his mouth and pointed his fork at Jack. "Who knows, Jackie boy? We might end up facing off each other again."

Nose scrunched up in disgust, I kicked Raiden under the table. "Swallow, then talk. And who says you will? Maybe it will be Firestar or even none of you at all."

Firestar threw an arm around the back of my chair and leaned in close. "Are you questioning our abilities? Or do you need a reminder of how capable we actually are?" The rumble that came from him caused me to shiver as it settled low between my thighs.

Rubbing them together, I leaned over toward him until our mouths were barely inches apart. My hand slid into his lap and played along the inside of his thigh, making his breath hitch. With a coy smile, I brushed my lips against his and murmured, "But do you know how capable I am?"

Firestar opened his mouth to answer, but my hand clamped down on his length, startling him so much that he jumped in his seat. His thighs hit the bottom of the table and knocked his cup over, spilling the cold liquid right into his lap.

Quickly moving away, I covered my mouth as I tried to stifle a laugh. Raiden and the rest of the table didn't bother, laughing and pointing at Firestar's predicament. Even Jack let out a chuckle.

Glaring down at his wet lap, Firestar turned his eyes to me. "Why you little minx ..." He reached for me, and I darted out of my seat, rounding the table to hide behind Raiden. "Don't think Raiden will save you this time."

I stuck my tongue out at him and ducked down beside Raiden's chair. Hands wrapped around my waist and I was lifted into the air with a screech. Raiden grinned up at me as he handed me off to Firestar.

"You traitor," I growled, kicking my legs hoping to hit something precious. "What happened to hoes before bros?"

"I think you have that backward, love." Raiden shook his head and laughed. "Besides, you have to admit that you deserve this. Just take your lickings like a good girl. Who knows? You might even like it."

My face flushed hotly at his words, a visual reminder that I had indeed liked the last spanking I'd gotten. Still, it didn't keep me from fighting tooth and nail as Firestar dragged me out of the dining room.

Firestar didn't take me to our room as I expected, but stopped us in the hallway beside a door I didn't recognize. Frowning, I started to ask where the heck we were, but Firestar didn't give me a chance. Shoved inside, I found myself in a linen closet.

Backing up until I was on the far side of the

little closet, I shook my head. "I don't even want to know how you even knew this was here. I just want to get this over with."

"Really now? I'm hurt." Firestar placed a hand on his chest with a fake pained expression.

"No, you're not," I countered, crossing my arms over my chest. "Nothing hurts you."

Firestar shook his head and moved on me. "Now that's where you are wrong. Many things hurt me, and most of those are from you."

My glare softened as my arms started to drop. That was the wrong thing to do. Firestar was on me in an instant, pinning my arms above my head and his hips trapping my own.

"You have been a very bad girl, Maya," he murmured against my face, causing those silly little tingles to reappear. "What am I going to do with you?"

My eyes fluttered shut as his mouth slid across my cheek, stopping briefly to nip at my earlobe before going lower. His hot breath caressed my skin before his mouth covered the junction between my neck and shoulder. As he sucked on the flesh there, I gasped and almost collapsed as my knees gave out on me. Firestar shifted so that one of his hands held mine while the other wrapped around my waist, keeping me upright.

"Not fair," I whimpered through his assault. I only had one weakness when it came to foreplay, one that Firestar knew and exploited often. There was no better way to rile me up quickly than to love-bite me. What that said about my personality I'd leave for my therapist to figure out, if I ever got one.

Releasing my neck, Firestar asked, "And what you did was fair?"

"No," I pouted, licking my lips as I tried to think of a way to appease him. "I was just playing around."

Firestar straightened back out, letting go of my hands to stroke my bottom lip. "There are so many better ways to play around than to damage something that gives you so much pleasure."

I snorted before I could help it. My hand shot up to cover my face, my eyes going wide. "I didn't mean that. I swear."

Shaking his head, Firestar smirked. "Just keep adding up the insults, and it might never find a way to pleasure you again."

"You don't mean that," I accused, calling his bluff.

"Don't I?"

"You'd really leave Jack and Raiden to pick up your slack?" I was playing with fire, I knew that, but I couldn't help it. He brought out the competitive side in me.

Firestar growled, his eyes flashing red. "No one can take my place, and I think it's about time you kiss and make up."

I cocked my head to the side, confused by what he said. He gave me no time to figure it out as his hands went to my shoulders and pushed. "On your knees."

Eyes widening, I glanced down at Firestar's pants and then back to his eyes. "Really? Right here?" I peeked around him to the closet door which didn't have a lock. "But anyone could walk in."

Lips curled up into a wicked grin, Firestar said, "Exactly."

I fought against my better nature telling me this was a bad idea. I wasn't an exhibitionist by any means, but I wasn't a prude either. If I was honest with myself, it wasn't the first time I'd done something naughty in a public place.

Sinking to my knees, I couldn't help the giddy

feeling that swept through me. I was really going to do this.

Eyes locked with Firestar's, I worked on his pants, the wetness from my lunch hijinks making it harder to undo them. When he was free, his length sprung out already hard and ready for me. Wrapping my hand around it, my hand was just big enough to touch fingertips. At least he wasn't as big as Jack. My jaw had ached for hours after that.

"What are you thinking about?" Firestar asked, knocking me out of my thoughts.

"Nothing," I muttered, my face heating. Now was not the time to compare my lovers' parts.

Tightening my grip on Firestar, I tested an upward stroke of my hand along his length. When Firestar groaned in response, I repeated it. I found a good rhythm that had Firestar gripping the shelf behind me, but just as I started to quicken my pace, Firestar stopped me.

"No, use your mouth." His hand curled into my hair and guided me toward his length. I opened my mouth and readily took him inside, sliding my tongue up and down him. Firestar's groans turned to gasps as I worked his length.

I swallowed as I came down on him, making the hand in my hair tighten almost painfully.

Moving back until I almost released him, I sucked hard on the tip. Firestar growled, his hand fisting my hair, urging me to keep moving. Not to disappoint, I continued my trek down until my lips bumped against his pubic bone. Slowly, I made my way back up him which Firestar didn't agree with.

The hand on my head started to direct me at a faster pace, his hips thrusting up into my mouth. Placing my hands on his legs, I let him direct me to his pleasure. I had to breathe quickly through my nose lest I pass out from lack of oxygen as the tip of Firestar hit the back of my throat.

The sounds he made caused a liquid heat to flow through my veins. There wasn't a sound in the world better than knowing you are causing your lover pleasure. Okay, so maybe the sound of bacon frying comes close, but it's still second. However, you measured it, those sounds were enough to make my heat slicken with need.

"Ah, Maya," Firestar groaned, "I can smell you."

To a human, that might sound a bit on the perverted side, but it only ramped up my need even more. I moved my mouth along him faster than before until I felt him tense above me. Relaxing my throat, I swallowed as much of him as I could until there wasn't anymore left.

Releasing him, I leaned back on my calves, admiring my work. Firestar stood breathlessly above me, a half-drunk expression on his face. Shifting out from beneath him, I headed for the door.

Firestar caught my hand before I could leave. "Wait. What about you?"

Smirking, I glanced down at his softening length. "I think you'll have to give me a rain check. Besides, I have others who can pick up your slack."

Laughing at Firestar's shocked expression, I darted out of the linen closet before he could retaliate. His roar filled the hallway as I made my way back to the dining room.

By the time I got back to my lunch, everyone else had already cleared the room, clearing my plate in the process. Frowning at the empty table, I almost sighed in relief when Carl showed up with my plate, still laden with food, in hand.

"I could just kiss you right now," I exclaimed as I grabbed the plate from his hands. Sitting down at the table, I devoured my meal like it was my last.

"Please don't." Carl held his hands up as if I might actually do it. "I like my head where it is, and your mates are quite territorial."

I snorted in agreement. "Don't I know it. Don't worry, I won't let them hurt you," I gave him a sly look "as long as you have some of those tarts available."

Carl laughed. "Of course, I do. But you better take them to go unless you want to miss the final fights."

My eyes widened as I realized he was right. For once, food could wait. I had to see who would win with my own eyes.

While the cook wrapped up a few tarts to take with me, I shoved one in my mouth. When the others safely in my hand, I raced out of the king's house. By the time I got there, the crowds had already gathered around the ring. From their jeers, it was apparent that either Raiden or Firestar was fighting.

I pushed my way through the crowd until I stood beside a pissed off Firestar and a worried Jack. "What'd I miss?"

They looked down at me with matching grimaces on their faces. Firestar growled in anger before gesturing at Jack. "I was late to the match, so Jack won by default."

"You did?" I asked, glancing at Jack.

"Yes, but that's not the problem." He pointed to

the ring. "That's the problem."

My eyes went from Jack to the ring where Raiden was fighting the largest man I'd ever seen. With a completely bald head, his menacing eyes just screamed death and destruction.

"They call him the Beast," Jack informed me with a frown. "He's from the farthest north village and new to the games."

"You've never seen him before?" I asked, still in awe at the massive man before us.

"No."

Jack's snippy answer didn't make me feel any better. I turned to Firestar and gestured toward his face. "What do you think of him?"

"He's definitely a tough opponent," Firestar grumbled. "The guy might be huge, but he's fast."

Not liking his answer, I became even more worried for Raiden who was barely standing at this point. His lip was busted open, and he was wavering on his feet. I didn't see him lasting much longer.

The crowd seemed to like it though. They cheered as the Beast put Raiden into a headlock, his ice powers covering his arms and shielding them from Raiden's lightning. Those massive arms squeezed, cutting off the oxygen to Raiden's brain.

As Raiden's face started to turn purple, I cried out, "He's going to kill him!"

Jack held me back from jumping into the ring. "No, he won't. It's an automatic forfeit if he kills his opponent."

I watched Raiden slowly lose consciousness, my heart pounding in my chest. But true to Jack's word, the moment Raiden went limp, the Beast released him, and the lightning dragon collapsed to the ground.

The crowd went wild as Lord Fafnir announced the Beast as the winner. A couple of medics grabbed Raiden and lifted him out of the ring. I rushed to his side, having to check for myself that he was still breathing.

I almost cried when I felt his chest rise and fall. A medic wiped his face clean before waving a piece of cloth in front of his nose that had a sharp medicinal smell to it. Raiden jerked awake, his arms flailing, and Jack pulled me back before I got hit accidentally. I didn't even realize he had followed me there.

"Where is he? I'll kill him." Raiden's eyes moved wildly in his head searching for an unseen opponent. When he realized he wasn't in the ring, he sank back on the ground with a groan. "Fuck. I've never lost so bad before."

"At least you got the chance to fight." Firestar smacked him on the leg.

"Pfft." Raiden rolled his eyes. "That only makes me feel worse."

13

————

Jack didn't look as happy as Firestar and Raiden were for him to fight the Beast. If anything, he looked worried.

For good reason.

The Beast had taken out Raiden easily enough, and I could tell Firestar wanted to see the ice dragon take a beating for winning by forfeit.

I, on the other hand, was worried for Jack. What could he possibly do to take out this massive mountain of a man? I just didn't see how he could win this one. If it had been me, I would have forfeited right when I saw the guy, but maybe I had less pride than they did.

Holding my breath as Lord Fafnir announced the final round which pitted Jack against the Beast,

I waited with the rest of the crowd for what was probably going to be a quick fight.

My heart beat rapidly as the fight started. Palms sweating, I wiped them on my pants as I tried to keep my nerves under control. A hand took mine and squeezed. I glanced down at the hand and then up to Raiden's face. He gave me an encouraging grin before turning back to the fight.

Jack wasn't fairing very well already. The Beast was indeed as fast as they said. He dodged everything Jack tried to hit him with. While Jack was quick in his own right, he wasn't quick enough to get out of the way of the Beast's football-sized fists. One of them clipped Jack on the side of the face hard enough to knock Jack back a couple steps.

"Ooh," the crowd and I both winced at the sound of the impact. That would definitely leave a bruise.

The beats lunged forward, obviously intending to end the fight. As he raised his hands high overhead to club Jack, the ice dragon flung out his hand. A wave of blue energy slammed into the beast, sheathing him in frost that seemed like it was nothing more than bits of cobweb.

Even still, the move slowed him enough for Jack to dodge, and as he gathered himself across the ring, the Beast smacked his fists together and growled.

His eyes glowed with sapphire light as his dragon came forth, and his wings sprouting on his back.

Massive and scary as hell were the only thoughts that came to my mind when I saw the Beast's wings. I'd never seen such large wings except on someone in actual full dragon form. Though, for his size, I'd imagine the Beast would need large wings to hold his weight.

Jack stood in awe for a moment at the sight of those wings. That ended up being just enough time for the Beast to grab him. Thick arms wrapped around Jack's middle, squeezing him tight. Jack pushed and twisted in place, trying to get loose of the Beast's immense, crushing strength.

I swore I heard something crack which was followed by a pained wince on Jack's face. I took a step forward without knowing it, but Firestar's hand fell on my shoulder to stop me. I wasn't going to go in there, and while I knew he wouldn't kill him, it still upset me to see Jack in so much pain.

No longer fighting the grip, Jack slacked in the Beast's arms, making the massive dragon think he'd won.

The Beast's eyes stopped glowing as his wings retracted. The crowd began to boo as he made to fling Jack across the ring. Only as the Beast shifted his grip, Jack's fist shot out, striking the Beast right in the throat.

The Beast dropped Jack, his meaty hands clutching at his neck as he tried to learn how to breathe again. Jack scrambled to his feet, one hand gripping his side, proof something was broken, but that wasn't going to stop him. Darting around the Beast, Jack jumped onto his adversary's back and wrapped his arms around the Beast's thick, bull-like neck.

The Beast tried to get Jack off his back, but his frame was so massive that he couldn't get his arms behind him with enough leverage to pry Jack loose. His eyes bulged in his head as Jack tightened his arms around his neck. In one last attempt to free himself, the Beast grabbed Jack's arms, trying to pry them free with sheer brute strength, but he held on tight. Soon, the Beast fell to one knee and then the other. His eyes fluttered a few times before he fell forward with a loud boom.

As soon as he was sure the Beast was out, Jack released his hold on him, staggering to his feet. Lord Fafnir jumped into the ring faster than I had seen the old man move during the entire time we had been here.

He grabbed Jack's hand and lifted it, and the movement made Jack cry out. Lowering Jack's arm with an apologetic frown, Lord Fafnir shouted, "We have our champion!"

The crowd went wild. Everyone must have expected the Beast to be crowned the champion. To be honest, if I had bet on this game, I would have lost big time. No way would anyone have guessed Jack would win. The fact that he did was a miracle, though I was sure he didn't feel that way now.

A medic helped Jack make his way over to where I stood. There was a pained grimace on his face that didn't bode well. The moment he was within touching distance, I clambered over to him. I searched him over, looking for more damage, but Jack waved me off.

"I'm fine, Maya." He groaned as the medic accidentally touched a tender spot. "I just need to get to Trina, that's all."

"Then I'll come with you." I took Jack's arm around and put it over my shoulder, the medic doing the same on the other side.

"You don't have to do that." Jack shook his head, trying to remove his arm from me. "You should stay and watch the race. Raiden and Firestar need someone to cheer for them."

My lips twisted in displeasure. "I'm sure they will manage without me this one time."

I hated to miss the next event. I'd have loved to see Firestar and Raiden race. Flying had always fascinated me, and now that I could fly myself, it intrigued me even more.

To see a whole group of dragons of all kinds race against the clock would be a magnificent sight to see. With how competitive Raiden and Firestar were with each other, I'd imagined it would be an even more entertaining sight.

I was sad to miss it, but Jack's injury couldn't wait. He might have won the event, but he had taken quite a beating to gain the title of champion.

"Yeah, Jack," Raiden added with a smirk. "You took enough of a beating for all three of us. You deserve our lovely Maya's full attention. I'm sure she can find some way to make you feel better." He waggled his eyebrows at us.

I rolled my eyes at him. Leave it to Raiden to be perverted at a time like this.

"Fine," Jack huffed, finally agreeing. I think it was more from the fact that he was in pain than actually wanting me to come. If I was hurting like he was, I didn't think I'd care who was at my side as long as they helped make the pain stop.

I tried my best not to jostle Jack as we made our way back to the house. Jack, the trooper that he was, barely made a sound the entire way. But one look at his sweat-covered face, and I knew he was in a lot of pain.

The medic pushed open the infirmary door and called for Trina. She came rushing toward us, took one look at Jack's face, and said, "On the table."

We brought Jack back to the main examination area. After helping him get up on the table, I didn't move from his side until Trina asked me to give her some space.

"I thought you won this thing all the time? Was this guy so different because of how massive he was?" I asked as Trina worked on him.

Thankfully, most of the blood didn't seem to be his own, but he still had a nasty gash on his forehead and from the way he winced under Trina's expert touches, probably a broken rib or two.

"I'm out of practice." Jack winced as Trina cleaned his wounds. "I usually spend months training before the games, but this time—"

"You were with me." I sighed. It seemed my endless amount of bad luck was contagious. "You probably should have sat this one out then, don't you think?"

Jack gave me an incredulous look. "Why would I do that? Just because I'm out of practice doesn't mean I couldn't win. I did, didn't I?"

"Yes, but it was stupid," Trina answered for me. She and I exchanged an understanding smile. I knew there was a reason I liked this woman.

"What she said." I narrowed my eyes at him. "You guys keep harping on me about being safe. That should go for you as well. Who's going to protect me if you guys get killed?"

Jack's brow furrowed at my assessment, for once not arguing with me. If they thought me getting hurt would be bad, losing one of them would be the end of me.

"Maya," Jack said my name with a soft tone. I glanced up to meet his eyes, and the knowing look there made me look away. "You aren't going to lose me. Not today, not ever."

My face flushed, and I grumbled, "What? Are you a mind reader?"

"No." Jack chuckled before using his uninjured arm to tip my chin up. "I just know you."

"Then you should know what I'm thinking right

now," I countered, remembering how much of a pretentious dick he could be.

Jack's eyes narrowed, and he leaned toward me, completely ignoring the fact that Trina was there. "You better watch your mouth, or I'll give it something better to do."

"And that would be my cue to leave," Trina announced, quickly getting to her feet. A faint blush covered her cheeks as she darted away, back to the games no doubt.

When she was gone, I moved closer to Jack, close enough that my nose brushed his. "In your shape, I don't think you are in the position to make me do anything, Jack." I punctuated his name with an over-exaggerated click of my tongue.

A deep, gurgling growl was my only warning before I found myself thrown over the side of the examination table. Jack's hard front ground into my backside making me groan. I tried to turn my head to glare back at him for his rough handling, but Jack's hand grabbed hold of my braid, keeping me still.

"You need to learn some manners, my love." Jack pressed into me with each word, causing me to squirm beneath him. I wanted nothing more than to have him take me right now, but the part of me that still stung from his earlier betrayal convinced me not to make it easy for him.

"I think you have that the wrong way," I snapped back, rubbing myself against him in circular movements. "I'm not the one who doesn't know when he is beat."

"From the position, I'm in," Jack said, his hand dragging up the bottom of my dress until the air hit my bare skin, "I'm not the one who is in denial."

The hand on my hair released me only to cup my breast instead. My skin sang at the contact even through the dress, my nipple pebbling instantly. Distracted by his hand, I didn't realize he had undone his pants until I felt the press of his head against my soaked folds. I rocked my hips backward, urging him to take me, but Jack refused. With one hand on my hip, he rubbed himself on my sensitive skin, coating himself with my wetness.

With my skirt above my waist, my front rubbed against the table, sending shocks of pleasure through my body. That pleasure only intensified as Jack maneuvered my legs further apart. I knew I was supposed to be making it hard for him, but the need inside of me said he had suffered enough. I had suffered enough. I should just let him put us both out of our misery.

As if reading my mind once more, Jack prodded at my entrance, only going in an inch before withdrawing. I mewled like a kitten begging for more. Thankfully, Jack wasn't in the withholding mood, because his next thrust slid him even further inside, ripping a gasp from me.

"Maya?" he asked with concern and a breaking restraint in his voice.

I swallowed and breathed, "I'm okay. Keep going."

That was all the encouragement Jack needed before he pulled back and then pushed into me once more, this time until his hips touched mine. Completely inside of me, the thickness of him took my breath away. I didn't have time to catch it before he was moving again. Each movement increased in speed until I was gasping for air, the overwhelming feeling of him almost too much to handle.

My orgasm hit me all at once, making me cry out and scratch at the table beneath me. My breathing came out in rapid pants as Jack grunted and shuddered above me. His hips stilled against me as his hand stroked my back. When he slipped from me, I could feel the residue from our lovemaking on my thighs and grimaced. I'd definitely need a shower after this.

"Are you, all right?" Jack asked, helping me pull my skirt back down and stand up.

"I'm good. Great even. I just need ..." My eyes searched the area for something to clean off with and landed on a stack of towels. They were probably meant for injuries, but they would do. Seeing where my gaze pointed to, Jack retrieved a towel and even went so far as to kneel before me to clean beneath my skirt. His slow movements against my hyper-sensitive skin almost had me orgasming again, but the moment was over all too soon.

"Are you ready to return to the public?" Jack asked, offering me his arm.

I took it with a goofy grin, completely at ease. "Lead the way, my champion."

As we exited the examination area and walked through the infirmary proper, my footsteps slowed. A feeling of dread filled me as I remembered where exactly we were and what we had just done. I dropped Jack's arm and rushed over to where Fujin and Raijin had last been recouping. I hoped against hope that they had recovered enough to be discharged from the infirmary. When I pulled back the curtain to their beds, and my eyes met their amused ones, I knew it had been too much to hope for.

"Uh..." I couldn't find the words to explain, but from the looks on their faces, I didn't need to. They had heard it all.

"What is it?" Jack asked, coming to my side. When he saw the grinning twins, he cursed under his breath. "How long have you two been in here?"

Fujin placed his hands behind his head and smirked. "The whole time."

"And what a time it was," Raijin added with a heated expression. "Now, I know why your men are so infatuated with you, Maya Rose."

My face flushed with embarrassment as I shifted in place. "Just don't tell anyone okay?" I fidgeted with my hands unable to meet their gazes now or ever again.

"Who would we tell?" Fujin answered with a shrug. "Besides, such matters are private and only meant for close company. And I have to say, Maya, I feel quite close to you now."

The twins' combined laughter only made my face burn hotter. Without a word, I turned on my feet and headed for the door. If I hurried, I might still see the end of the race, and hopefully, it would be enough to erase my mortification.

I doubted it though.

If the twins were anything like their brother,

they weren't going to let it go just because I asked. They might keep it a secret, but they'd find a way to torture me with it. I'd just have to keep my distance from the pair for the foreseeable future, or at least until they find someone else to tease.

14

By the time I got back to the square, the race was over. People were gathered around the winners, clapping them on the back and chattering about the race.

I searched for two familiar heads or their red and black scales, but Raiden and Firestar were nowhere to be found. Who I did find was Gretchen. She stood beside two other men with similar features to hers. I could only assume they were her brothers or some other close relatives. The way they glared at me told me she had told them who I was and what I'd done.

Or rather what she thought I had done to her. It was hardly my fault her mate had accepted his uncle's request. Though, I knew no matter how much I explained it, she would never believe me. I'd always be the woman who stole her love, which meant she was dangerous.

"Maya." I turned away from the scorned woman to see Firestar and Raiden approaching me. Men and woman clapped them on the backs as they made their way through the crowd. It was plain that I was not the only one who had an eventful last few hours.

"So," I started, grinning up at them, "who won?"

Raiden smirked, and Firestar scowled before the former announced a bit too gleeful, "We both did."

My brow furrowed. "Huh?"

"We tied," Firestar grumbled, his arms over his chest and his eyes off to the side. Out of the two, he seemed the most upset about it. That was not surprising really.

"Yep." Raiden punctuated his affirmative with a pop as he adjusted his pants. "The others had no chance. After the first half hour, it was only Firestar and me at the front."

"I would have won," Firestar growled, shoving Raiden with a hand, "if you hadn't cheated."

Raiden placed a hand on his chest, his mouth

hanging open in innocent surprise. "I did no such thing. You are just a sore loser."

I giggled as they argued over who really won. From what they were saying, I really regretted missing the race, but an ache between my thighs reminded me of what I got in return.

"What's that look for?" Raiden asked, quirking a brow at me. His and Firestar's eyes swept over me before they broke into knowing grins. "You and Jack made up."

Tucking my hair behind my ear, I ducked my head. "We might have."

"Good." Firestar wrapped an arm around my shoulders, bringing me into his warmth. "We have enough troubles without losing one of our best fighters."

"And her feelings had nothing to do with it?" Raiden asked with a disbelieving shake of his head. That shake froze when his gaze caught something that made his expression turn to worry. "You need to watch your back, Maya. If I know anything, there is nothing worse than a woman with a grudge against you."

I followed his gaze to where Gretchen stood. I'd had the same thought, but with Raiden's warning, I knew I wasn't being over cautious. There would be a time I would have to deal with Gretchen. I just hoped it wouldn't end badly for either of us.

"When's the next event?" I asked, changing the subject to something less worrying. "I still get to participate right?"

"Yes." Firestar sighed, not at all pleased with the situation.

"But first," Raiden said, pulling me from Firestar's embrace to his, "we feast and celebrate my great victory."

"You mean our," Firestar growled in my ear as he latched himself to my other side. Shoved between their two bodies, I was almost too warm as they led me back to the house.

"Sure, sure." Raiden laughed and rolled his eyes. "But only the real winner gets to accompany Maya tomorrow during the hunt."

"Tomorrow?" I asked, curious to know why there was going to be a delay in the contests, then my eyes found the horizon. Pink and orange painted the skies, making me realize how late it actually was. There'd be no use in starting now unless I wanted to hunt at night, which I didn't.

"Bright and early," Raiden explained and then winked. "Maybe we should skip the party and go straight to bed?" He wagged his eyebrows up and down making me laugh.

"What makes you think she will be bedding you tonight, cheater?" Firestar taunted, jerking me to the other side of him. I was glad to no longer be between them - surprising I know - but knew that getting in the way of their rivalry would only end in bloodshed.

Raiden only grinned at Firestar's words, not affected at all by his name calling. "Well, we could always share her, as we did the race."

The thought of those two sharing me caused a visceral reaction. Jack and Raiden had shared me before, but I never expected Firestar to, now or ever. He had too much ego to not be the main attraction. The thoughtful look on Firestar's face said he might actually be considering it.

"Guys," I murmured, noticing the people gathering around us. We were standing in the middle of the hallway, blocking everyone's path. "Can we not discuss our sex life in public? I've had about all the exhibition I can handle for one day."

Firestar and Raiden gave me a curious look, but I wasn't about to admit what happened in the infirmary. There was no need to relive my humiliation.

Thankfully, I was saved from the questions

because Jack came through the crowd. My face lit up until I saw Fujin and Raijin close behind him. I had wondered why he had stayed behind after I had left. I shot the twins warning looks, but they only grinned in return.

"I hear you two won," Jack said, not noticing my uncomfortable glances toward the twins.

Raiden opened his mouth to answer, but Firestar shoved him shutting him up before he could. "I won. *He* cheated."

And so, the argument started again.

By the time we made it to the dining hall where the festivities were being held, everyone else had already filed in. Firestar and Raiden still argued about who had won, while Jack stayed close to my side.

My eyes darted to the twins who seemed to take great joy in watching me squirm as I waited for them to say something. Jack took my hand in his and drew me around to him. I pulled my eyes away from the twins with a sigh.

"Something is bothering you," Jack stated, his pale eyes filled with worry. I glanced at Fujin and Raijin and then back to Jack. "Ah, I see. You are worried they will tell someone about our ... time together." Jack slid his hands around my waist and smiled slightly. "Do not worry. After you left, I gave them a sound threat that they would not dare to test."

"You did?" I cocked a brow, surprised that he would be thoughtful enough to do so.

Jack tilted my chin up and pressed his lips to mine. "Do you think any of us want anyone else to hear your cries of pleasure?"

I shrugged a shoulder. "I didn't think you really minded."

"I don't care about myself," Jack explained with a soft expression. "I do care about my mate being embarrassed. So, do not worry. They will keep their mouths closed."

"But will they keep them closed around me?" I muttered, more to myself than to Jack, but he answered anyway.

"That I cannot promise you, but with this …" He paused and withdrew the blade he had given me, the one I had tossed on the table in front of Gretchen before I knew the whole story. "You can administer a threat of your own. Perhaps something a bit closer to home?"

I laughed at his suggestion and took the blade from him. In my dress, I didn't really have anywhere to put it. I had opted for flats rather than boots this time, but still, I felt safer with it in my grasp.

"Thank you," I sighed into his embrace. "I am sorry I tossed it away so easily."

Jack caressed my face with a solemn smile. "There will never be a need to again."

"Definitely," I agreed.

"Come, let us celebrate our men's victory and later we can find a more pleasurable place to celebrate alone." Jack wrapped his arm around my shoulders and led me to the tables.

"Get in line. Those two have been fighting over the honor since they won." I laughed, pointing at Firestar and Raiden. "I can't figure out if it's because they actually want me or want to outdo each other."

Jack held my chair out for me with a grin. "Probably a bit of both."

I nodded in agreement as I took my seat. This time our table was full of familiar faces, none of which who would stab me in the back for a misunderstanding. My men, the twins, and Jack's cousin, Tyrell, sat around me, laughing and eating as if there wasn't a war brewing. I wished I could forget so easily.

"You know," Tyrell said after a moment, "my

cousin has never smiled so much in his life. Until he met you, that is." His lips curved up in what could have been a smile of his own but also could have been a grimace.

"Really?" I ducked my head, my own mouth tipping up. "I would think he would have plenty to smile about here."

"Not so." Tyrell shook his head. "We might be a close-knit village, but we still have our share of problems. Take your father's invitation, for example."

I felt Jack stiffen beside me, but he didn't stop Tyrell from continuing his story.

"It had originally been meant for me, but my father didn't want to give your father the satisfaction of merging our kingdoms. Not that I could blame him." Tyrell took a bite of his meat, his mouth too full to say anymore.

"Well." I smiled tightly. "It all worked out for the best. Jack is dear to me, and I wouldn't trade him for all the land in Waesigar."

"Then you will be a much better ruler than your father." Lord Fafnir appeared at the end of the table with a straight face. Silence fell over us all as every gaze fixed on the lord.

I gave a wry grin. "I cannot disagree with you

there. I fear my father and many others have lost sight of what is best for the people and care only for what is best for themselves."

Jack squeezed my hand next to me in reassurance. At least, I wasn't the only one who thought so.

"I, for one, am glad you and our Jack have done so well for yourselves. Firestar and Raiden as well." Lord Fafnir glanced at the others who nodded in appreciation. "It is hard enough to find love in our world let alone with so many. I hope for happiness and a healthy child for you all."

"Thank you, my lord." I bowed my head slightly, thrilled that at least someone wished us well. The others murmured their own thanks before Lord Fafnir announced his departure. With him gone, the table relaxed once more.

"So, about tomorrow's hunt," Raiden started, pointing his fork at me, "who do you wish to come with you?"

"No one." I stared him down, daring him to argue with me. He didn't have to though because Jack turned me to him with a worried expression.

"Maya, you cannot go on this hunt alone."

"Why not? I can take care of myself."

"True," Jack agreed. The tone of his voice made me know a but was coming. "But it is a long hunt. It lasts all day, and you might get too tired to return on your own. Wouldn't you feel better to have someone by your side to take you home if you find it is too much for you?"

"But I won't." I shook my head. "You guys are always with me. Protecting me. I need to be able to prove to myself that I can do something on my own." I glanced at the three of them. "I love you, and I understand your concern, but I can't do that with you babysitting me."

Jack exchanged a look with the others and sighed. "Very well, if that is your wish."

"Yes!" I practically danced in my seat.

"But," Firestar interjected, interrupting my happy dance, "we will all be participating as well to keep an eye on you. So, if something happens …"

"It won't," I assured him.

"*But*, if it does," Firestar continued, ignoring my glare. "We will be close by if you need us."

Thinking about it for a moment, I considered their conditions. They weren't really letting me go alone, but they weren't going to hover over me like nagging hens. I supposed it was the best I was going to get in my condition. Beggars couldn't be choosers.

"Fine," I sighed in defeat before holding a finger up. "You can follow me, but not too close."

The guys nodded in agreement though none of them looked very happy about it. With the decision made, I clapped my hands together like a giddy child. "So, what are we hunting?"

15

I went to bed alone that night and woke up the next day bright and early. I showered quickly and started for the bedroom door when a wave of sickness came over me.

"No, not today," I groaned as I darted back to the bathroom.

My stomach heaved, but since I had nothing inside, it was only dry heaves. To me, that was even worse. Acid coated my throat and tongue, making my nausea worse. God, why did it have to happen today of all days? I groaned and sat beside the toilet, my hand on my face.

I sat there for a while, letting my stomach settle, and almost didn't hear the knock on my door. It opened before I could ask who it was, and the sound of three sets of feet entered.

Great. Just what I needed. If the guys saw me like this, they wouldn't let me compete today.

"Maya," Raiden called out, his voice coming closer to the bathroom.

I jumped to my feet and regretted it instantly, my world spinning around me. Gritting my teeth, I forced myself to stand straight, my hand on the sink. I turned the water on and faced away from the door to give me time to get a hold of myself.

"Maya," Raiden said once more with a breath of relief. "Why didn't you answer?"

I took a handful of water into my mouth and swished it around before glancing over my shoulder. "I was using the bathroom. As much as I care for you, I would like to keep some mystery in this relationship."

Raiden's nose wrinkled, but he didn't comment. "We were coming to see if you wanted to get some breakfast before the hunt. Don't want to be out there on an empty stomach, especially with the competition so fierce today."

"Are you worried?" I asked, following him out of the bathroom where Jack and Firestar waited. They were all dressed for the hunt already. Even

Jack had opted to wear pants and a shirt rather than his usual nice suit. I didn't blame him. Traipsing through the woods would have ruined it.

"We don't want you to get hurt is all." Jack approached, holding out the clothing he had picked out for me. "Are you sure you want to do this?"

I didn't really, now that my stomach had decided it wanted to dance. But I'd made a big fuss over it. My pride wouldn't let me back out now. "Yes, I'm sure."

Firestar gave me a disbelieving look, but he didn't out me to the others. I slipped into the thick pants and long-sleeved shirt Jack had provided me. The boots he brought were different than my usual. The insides were lined with fur and would keep me warm during the hunt but didn't have much room for my dagger to hide.

I held the dagger in my hand, trying to figure out where to put it when Firestar stepped forward. He bent down, his hands grinding around my thigh and making me think was trying to start something. Before I could protest one way or the other, he stood back up. In the place of his hands was a snug strap with a sheath for the dagger.

Sliding the dagger into it, I was ready. Physically

that was. Mentally I just wanted to crawl back into bed. Why did I fight to do this again?

"Now, how about breakfast?" Raiden suggested, leading us to the bedroom door. "You want to have as much strength as possible for today. You can't take much of anything else with you."

"Why not?" I cocked my head to the side. "This is a hunt. Usually, people bring provisions."

"Ah, but this is also a race," Jack reminded me. "If you ever hope to win, you won't have much time to stop and eat or rest."

"Explain to me again why we are hunting a piece of metal instead of a deer or something?" I asked as we made our way to the kitchens.

"Because that wouldn't be fair to the deer, for one," Jack explained with great care. "For another, it is easier to know for sure who won without much cheating when hunting an object and not something living."

"Well, it wouldn't be alive at the end of it," I chuckled, but they didn't laugh with me. Bunch of stiffs.

We didn't stop to eat with the rest of the visitors but went straight to the kitchen. The lovely cook, Carl, had a care package ready for us, letting me know the guys had already thought ahead.

"Come." Firestar held out his hand to me, the basket in the other hand. "We want to have a meal with you that doesn't end in an argument for once."

"Fat chance of that happening." I snorted and rolled my eyes. I ignored the eyes on us as we left the dining room. Gretchen and her crew were still upset with me. I just hoped they weren't planning to compete as well.

Pushing her from my mind, I followed the men to a small balcony. It was covered in glass so that while the sky was visible, the cold couldn't get through. Outside, the sun had only just come over the horizon, and the mixture of colors was so dazzling that I was lost for a moment.

"Pretty," I murmured as I sat down at the small table with the other three. They handed out plates and raspberry tarts as well as a hot pot of chamomile tea.

I glanced up from my cup, a question on my tongue, but Firestar answered before I could ask it. "Carl suggested you might like some to settle your stomach."

Nodding at that, I continued to sip from my cup as I enjoyed the sunrise. It had to be one of the first moments in a while that I could just enjoy my meal with all my men around me. No drama. No fighting. Just pure happiness.

Far too soon, we finished our meals and couldn't delay any longer. The hunt would start soon, and if I still wished to participate, I would need to be in place.

"Are you sure you still want to do this?" Raiden asked as the guys ushered me toward the gathering spot.

The group waiting was quite a bit bigger than I expected. It seemed like everyone who had come, whether they participated in the first two games or not, was going to try their luck at this one. Sadly, that included Jack's ex-lover, Gretchen.

Her pale hair was plaited into two braids but noticeably lacking any decorations. Her brown pants clung to her hips and thighs, far more muscular than my own. I really should start training more seriously. Though now that I was pregnant, I doubted my keepers would let me.

Wrinkling my nose at the woman who had once held my Jack's heart, I turned back to Raiden with an arched brow. "Why are there so many people here? I didn't expect so much competition."

"I can answer that." Jack cleared his throat and stepped closer to me, clearly uncomfortable. My gaze shot back to Gretchen who had spotted us, a tortured look on her face that I knew well. She still loved him. That much was clear. It only made her even more dangerous.

"The item we are hunting down isn't just some trophy declaring the winner. It's also made of pure gold." His eyes flickered to me as if expecting me to be surprised, but I only stared at him, waiting. "It might not seem like a big deal to you, but there are plenty of people here who would kill for that kind of treasure."

I didn't doubt that. Human or dragon alike, when it came to money, morals usually went out the window. Suddenly, Gretchen wasn't my only threat in this hunt.

Turning my attention away from Jack and back to the other competitors, I saw that there were more men than women. Maybe it was a hint I shouldn't be there, but then again, I'd never been one to take a hint. The intimidating looks being shot my way told me that the other competitors didn't know that.

Ignoring them, I adjusted my thigh strap, so it wasn't cutting off the blood to my center, not that I really needed it right now. Sex was the last thing on my mind right, but apparently, I was one of the only ones.

Those who weren't trying to get me to drop out had something else entirely on their minds. The eyes boring into me were not those of someone taking in the competition. One look at some of the males around me made me grimace. There were far too many interested eyes on me, and the leers I received weren't completely about sex either. Something told me the rumors about me had indeed reached the far north.

"So, a pure gold what?" I asked, shrugging off the varied looks coming my way. "A stag? Or maybe even a dragon egg?" I snorted with a roll of my eyes. Like dragons laid eggs. I couldn't imagine squatting one of those out. Talk about ouch.

"Actually," Jack drew out, sliding a hand around my waist and pulling me flush against his side, his voice by my ear, "it's a dragon." He pushed my braid to one side, his lips brushing my neck. I let out a shiver, not understanding the sudden closeness but not complaining either.

"Why a dragon?" I murmured, slowly turning around to meet Jack's gaze. With a hint of a smile, I placed a hand on his chest, loving the feel of him beneath my palm. "Isn't that a bit cliché?"

Jack leaned forward until his lips caressed mine. "Not when it could feed your village for a year." He captured my mouth with his in a searing kiss, but before I could sink into it, I was jerked away from him and into Firestar's arms.

"Hey!" I cried out, smacking him on the arm. "What's the big idea?"

The fury on Firestar's face confused me. Our conversation couldn't have elicited such a reaction. Even the public display of affection wouldn't cause his annoyance, not unless Firestar had a change of heart he hadn't let me know about.

"Ask him." Firestar glared at Jack.

My gaze shot back to Jack who had a guilty expression his face. He wouldn't meet my eyes, and my stomach sank through my butt. My eyes locked on to Gretchen who watched us with a hurt in her face. Now, I was the one who was hurt.

"I can't believe you," I growled, stepping toward Jack. "I forgave you for your deception, but that doesn't mean I'm okay with you using me to get Gretchen off your case." Jack's shoulders rose up to his ears at my accusation. Good. He should feel bad. "If you want people to stop seeing you as an ice king, maybe you should stop acting like you don't have a heart."

"Maya," Jack started, pain in his voice.

I held my hands up, stopping him as I shook my

head. "I've changed my mind. I'm going to do this on my own." Firestar and Raiden tried to interrupt me, but I stopped them. "No, don't even."

With a huff, I stomped away from them as Raiden snarled at Jack, "Not cool, man."

Stopping at a less dense part of the group, I crossed my arms over my chest and waited. I could feel the eyes on me, but I refused to let them bother me. I was tired of being the weak link in our group, tired of being used by everyone who thought I was their meal ticket to greater power. I wanted to be the one who came out on top for once.

My hand went to my stomach, and I closed my eyes. I tried to hear the heartbeat Trina had revealed to me before, but no matter how hard I strained, I couldn't hear it. I sighed heavily, tensing as a presence stopped beside me.

"What do you want?" I said wearily, not even bothering to look at my visitor. The hunt hadn't even started, and I was already tired, not a good omen for my chances of winning.

"He'll never stay, you know." Gretchen apparently didn't notice my lack of gusto or just didn't care. "You're just a blip in his rise to power, and once he has it, he'll toss you aside like the worthless slut you are."

Usually, those words would cause some sort of fiery anger or even annoyance to rise in me, but I was all out of feelings for the day. I only had one thing on my mind, and that was winning this hunt and showing everyone that I didn't need protecting, that I could stand on my own.

"Is that all?" I rolled my eyes, a bored tone to my voice.

Gretchen scoffed, clearly not expecting my reaction. "You have no shame, do you?"

I turned my head, finally looking at her, a nasty grin on my lips. "Why should I be ashamed? I've done nothing wrong. As far as I'm concerned, you are the only one who should be ashamed. Jack left you for someone better, and you don't have the brains to know when you should bow out."

"I'm not the one stringing along three men." Gretchen's voice rose a pitch, drawing some attention toward us. "Some dragons might be okay with that kind of thing, but I believe in love with one true mate. But look at you, taking all three when you couldn't even get one without your father behind you."

"Which is it, Gretchen?" I sighed, shifting my body around to face her. "Am I a slut or undesirable? Because the two don't really go together."

My words caused a growl to rumble from Gretchen, and my hand went straight for the hilt of my dagger. Gretchen's eyes locked onto it and her lips curled into a wicked grin.

"Enjoy my dagger while you can because I will be getting it back from you soon." Her spittle splashed on my face, and I resisted the urge to wipe it away. Instead, I took a step closer to her.

"The only way you are getting this dagger back is when I shove it through your frigid heart."

The glow of magic in her eyes was the only warning I had before she came at me, a roar ripping from her throat. Her hands barely touched my shoulders when another voice boomed louder than Gretchen's outraged cry.

"Ladies and gentlemen, welcome to the final game of this season," Lord Fafnir announced, freezing our fight in its tracks.

With a snarl, Gretchen shoved me away from her and headed back toward her group, her attention temporarily off of me. For how long that would last, I didn't know. I did know she wouldn't give up, not with love on the line.

16

I didn't need to turn to know my guys were watching me. They'd stayed away from me for now, but I wouldn't bet they'd stay away when the hunt started. With the way Gretchen had it in for me, it was probably a good thing.

"I want you all to know how proud I am to have so many participants this year. You have honored us with your presence." Lord Fafnir smiled and nodded around the group. His eyes eventually landed on Jack and warmed. "I am especially over-joyed that my favorite nephew has rejoined us for this season, along with his lovely mate."

Everyone's eyes fell on Jack, whose smile seemed more like an attempt not to throw up. I noticed a few mutters and confused eyes cast my way, but I refused to acknowledge them. It was none of their business why I was standing over here and Jack over there, or why they were letting their pregnant mate enter the hunt by herself. It was nobody's business but ours. Right?

Lord Fafnir seemed to notice I was standing away from Jack and the others because his expression wilted for a moment before it came back. He gave me a curious look but said nothing more before he went back to his speech. "The hunt will last until someone finds the trophy. Whether it be one hour or one week, we will have our champion!"

The crowd lifted up in a roar of agreement, their feet pounding, and hands raised above their heads. The tip of my lips curved up, unable to keep a frown with all of the excitement around me. The fight between Jack and me fell to the back of my mind as the need for the hunt raced through my veins. I hadn't been this ecstatic for something since Ryan and I first learned that our bosses had accepted the proposal for the Waesigar video game. Suddenly, I couldn't wait to get my feet off the ground.

"On my mark." Lord Fafnir raised a hand in the air, and the bodies around me tensed, everyone lining up together in preparation to run. I found myself shifting my weight, my hands clenched into fists at my sides as I readied to propel myself forward. My line of sight locked on the trees before us, but out of my eye, I watched and waited for Lord Fafnir's hand to fall. As if in slow motion, it fell to his side, and he called out, "Begin!"

My feet raced across the ground, my arms pumping at my sides. A horde of us bolted for the trees, most of us not paying any mind to the others, everyone too focused on the hunt. Still, there were a few that were more interested in taking out the competition than winning fairly.

One, a man with a wicked scar down one side of his face, came at me. I dodged to the right as he dove for me, missing me by an inch. I didn't look back to see if he was coming for me again. I kept my eyes on the trees only a few feet away from me.

Something flew past me, the wind of it catching my hair and I glanced back briefly to see the man on the ground with a familiar redhead beating him to a pulp. I should have stopped and yelled at Firestar, but I didn't. My feet kept moving beneath me though I had no idea where I was going or where to even start.

I didn't know this land, and the white snow that covered the ground made it impossible to pick up any kind of scent. The other competitors, those from the north, didn't seem as lost as I was and quickly dispersed into the belly of the woods. I fumbled around for about half an hour, not really knowing where I was heading. I'd broken away from the main part of the group but still saw one or two people every few minutes. Catching my breath, I slowed to a walk, moving along an iced-over river.

It was actually really nice out here once you got used to the freezing temperature and the mush beneath your feet. The green pine trees were tall, and their boughs were full of snow. I didn't under-stand it, really. You'd think with how cold it was that nothing could stand to live in it. It was no wonder that those who lived in it became just as cold as their surroundings.

Irritation filled me as Jack's face came to my mind. Really, what was he thinking? How would he ever think that in the realm of all that was decent that using me to hurt his ex would ever be okay? I mean, yeah, if I wanted to get back at my ex, I might rub my hot new guy in their face, but the way that Gretchen and Jack made it sound, he was the one who dumped her. If anyone should be trying to hurt the other, it should be her.

"It doesn't make any sense," I scoffed and shook my head.

"Talking to yourself now? You might want to get that checked out."

My eyes shot from the river to follow the voice of Gretchen, who stood like the alpha bitch she thought she was, smirking at her own joke. The dagger was in my hand before I even thought about it, the point glinting in the sunlight.

"What do you want now?" I growled, my fingers tightening on the hilt.

"To finish what we started, of course." Gretchen laughed as her canines sharpened and she flexed her fingers, her nails lengthening to claws. Pale blue scales appeared down the side of her face as her eyes glowed a menacing blue.

I swallowed hard. Only the strongest of us could change completely to dragon form and just below that were those who could half shift. That was great for her, but shit for me.

"Hey, come on now. We can talk this out," I laughed nervously as Gretchen prowled toward me. My eyes darted around, searching for something or someone to put between me and the she-bitch. Where were my overprotective mates when I needed them?

"You think you are some kind of hot shit, don't you?" Gretchen snarled, swiping out at me.

I jumped back, barely dodging the sharp edges of her claws. Before she could attack me again, I lunged at her with the dagger. The point caught her in the arm, cutting a bloody gouge through her shirt.

Gretchen cried out and stumbled backward clutching the wound. "You bitch!"

"Takes one to know one!" I shouted, turning on my heels. So, running wasn't the bravest thing for me to do. I wasn't a coward, but I wasn't stupid. I knew when to fight and when to run, and this was definitely a time to run.

"Stupid, stupid Jack," I muttered and then growled. "Didn't think to tell me your ex-beau was a bad ass? That would have been helpful information."

"Still talking to yourself?" Gretchen cackled, closer to me than I expected.

Startled by that closeness, my feet tangled and flew out from under me. I crashed to the ground before I could stop myself and then she was on me. A sharp pain went through my scalp as my head was jerked back by my hair. I reached back and scratched at the hand holding me with my nails, my other hand lashing out blindly.

I must have caught something because the hand gripping my hair released. Turning over quickly, I shoved my feet out, planting them into Gretchen's chest and shoving her further away from me.

An idea suddenly came to me. Of course, my magic. Why was I trying to beat her with brute force? I kicked ass against those raiders in the east. Why should this ice bitch be any different?

I reached down into the earth, willing it to come to my aide. My brow furrowed when nothing happened. I tried again, searching for some form of life in the earth to help me. "What the fu-?"

In my confusion, I missed Gretchen coming up on me. Bent over and wide open, it was no surprise really when her claws slashed across my back, tearing cloth and skin alike. Letting out a startled gasp of pain, I stumbled forward, falling onto the iced-over river. Groaning, I twisted around as I tried to get away from Gretchen and her lethal touch.

The moment her boot landed on the ice, there was a threatening crack. Gretchen jumped back from the ice as if it had bitten her.

I let out a pained laugh at the terror on her face. "Scared of water, are we?"

Gretchen snarled and started for me once more, but the ice cracked beneath her foot, making her boot sink into the water. She scurried back out of the river, but not before her movements caused a chain reaction, first a small crack then a larger one as the whole ice sheet began giving out beneath me. My eyes widened, and I tried to summon my wings to get off the ice and into the air, but I wasn't fast enough. The last thing I saw was Gretchen's grinning face as I sank into the freezing water.

Pain raced across my back as I tried to swim to the surface. Cold poured through me, freezing me to the bone. I forced back the agony and pushed to the top only to be met with more ice. Panic rose in me as the current pulled me further down the river while I tried to beat my way through the seemingly endless ice capping it.

I fought against the current, trying to find an opening to break free to the surface. My lungs burned as the need to breathe turned from urgent desire to burning necessity. I'd never been a great swimmer to begin with, and I didn't know how much longer I could hold my breath.

Oh, my God, what about my child? The icy waters might hurt him or her, and let's not even think about the possibility of me drowning. Oh,

God. I needed to get out of here. I couldn't die like this. I still had to make Jack grovel for my forgiveness and then have crazy make-up sex. Ugh. Of course, I'd be thinking about sex at a time like this. Stupid freaking hormones. *I'm going to die!*

The darkness started to close in around me, and I knew then that I wouldn't make it. I'd never see Raiden's smiling face again, Firestar blowing up about something Raiden did, or even Jack trying so hard not to laugh at Raiden's jokes. I'd never know what it would be like to hold my child in my arms, to be a mother. I knew that I'd have been a good one. A damned good one.

Ned would be happy though. I'd be out of his way finally. Would my father just hand the kingdom over to him? Would he even mourn me?

Ryan and Bianca would never know what happened to me. I knew none of my family would care to go back and let them know. I'd just be their best friend who never came back. No Waesigar 2 for me.

Just as I began to give up hope, my head bounced against the hard ice once, twice, and then suddenly it broke the surface. I gasped for air, coughing as water spurted from my burning lungs. My arms flailed around me as I tried to stay above the water and not be pulled back beneath. The water blurred my vision, but I could still see bits and pieces. My fingers didn't touch any more ice, and I took that as a sign that I might be able to get to land.

When my feet touched the surface, and my head stayed above the water, I could have cried. I dragged myself to the shore, my body shivering and my lungs on fire. From the little I could see, there wasn't any sign of Gretchen, which was a relief. There also wasn't any sign of anyone else. The trees were barren here. All the pretty green pines gone. I instantly wanted them back.

Wrapping my arms around myself, I wondered what to do now?

17

Holy fuck balls, it was cold! I'd thought the temperature here was brutal before, but after a dip in the cold river, it was even worse. Even with the leather and fur lined clothing, now soaked through, I could feel every frigid gust of wind as if I were butt naked.

"What am I going to do now?" I muttered, glancing around. I couldn't stay where I was unless I wanted to freeze to death. If I'd been human, I'd have already died of hypothermia. "Thank God for little favors."

I searched the area once more, really taking it in now that my vision had cleared. Sadly, nothing had really changed. There were a lot of barren trees, and the ground was littered with branches. Those could be used for a fire but wouldn't do much good against the harsh wind.

As if on cue, another burst of cold air bashed into me, hitting me right in the back. I cried out and grimaced at the brutal reminder of the wound. I supposed I'd have to take care of that too.

But first some fire.

Easing up from the ground, I headed toward the trees and painstakingly gathered an arm full of wood. By the time I was done, my back was on fire, and my teeth were chattering. Trying to keep moving to hold off the cold, I scoured the area for the densest part of the woods, anything to protect against the piercing wind.

Piling the wood up, I grabbed a rock and reached for my dagger. When my hand touched the empty thigh sheath, panic gripped my heart. Where did it go? I stood to my feet and searched the area. It had to be here somewhere. I couldn't lose it too.

I fumbled through the woods, searching the ground for the silver glint of the dagger until I came back to the edge of the river. That's when I remembered. I'd had the dagger in my hand when I was fighting Gretchen, and when I fell into the water, it must have fallen from my hand when I got swept away.

While I knew now where the dagger had gone, that knowledge didn't make it appear on the banks of the river. More than likely, it had been taken even further down the river, and I wasn't going to find it on my own anytime soon. Part of me wanted to look for it anyway, but I knew I was better off using my energies to get warm, though it killed me to do so.

Making it back to my little bundle of wood, I tore a strip of leather from the hem of my shirt and tied it to a curved branch to make a bow. Then I took the straightest, pointiest stick I could find and used it for the bit in my crude bow drill. I wasn't the best camper, I'd left most of the tent and fire making to the guys, but after several minutes of effort, I managed to create a coal. Transferring it to a small pile of dead pine needles, I blew on it until I thought my lungs were going to give out.

Smoke poured into my face, burning my eyes and making me want to give up, but I persisted anyway, and another minute or so later, flames flickered to life.

I couldn't quite explain how happy seeing those flames made me. I had made fire. Sure, maybe Firestar could have lit it with a thought, but for me? This was great. Sure, I'd have rather not been out here at all, but as I put the flames beneath the crude wooden teepee of sticks and kindling I'd constructed and watched it eat into them before roaring to life, I was so happy I could scream.

It wasn't long before I was sitting beside a fire large enough to actually feel the warmth. I scooched closer to it, putting my hands out toward the flames. Normally, I'd have taken my clothes off to let them dry, but the wind still came through the trees less harshly than before, and I didn't want to chance the cold against my bare skin.

When I was able to feel my toes again, I reached back and gently prodded at the scratches on my back. My hand didn't come back bloody, but the wounds still stung like a mother. I'd no doubt have a scar by the time it healed, but I'd live.

Glancing up at the sky, I noticed the sun had only just now reached its highest peak. The was no chance of me winning the hunt now, not with my injury especially since I had no idea where I was. I could almost be to the next village, for all I knew. It was hard to keep track of where I was when I was fighting not to drown.

Letting out a huff of defeat, I laid down on the ground to rest. I rolled over, so my back was to the fire. That warmed and dried the back of my clothing but made me wince whenever the heat washed over my wounds. My mind wandered as I waited for my body to warm through.

The guys were probably freaking out. I hadn't been able to tell if they were following me after that initial fight, but I had been sure they'd keep close to me. But if they had been, Gretchen wouldn't have attacked me, or at least when she had, I would have had a backup.

No doubt they were blaming themselves for my disappearance, if they noticed at all. For all, I knew they might think I was still in the race and doing my best to hide from them. There goes my pride, screwing me over once more. Now, I'd die in the woods by myself because I made them think I didn't need them.

I sniffled as I curled around myself. I wouldn't cry. This wasn't a crying time. Okay, so maybe it was. Still, I had no one to blame but myself. My eyes burned as tears threatened to fall. I didn't fight them too hard, and before I knew it, I was bawling my eyes out. Like ugly wracking sobs that made my back hurt.

After I had a good cry, I realized how tired I really was. Fighting for one's life was exhausting work. Maybe I could just rest my eyes for a few minutes. The fire should last for a bit longer, but even so, I threw a few logs on the coals, anyway. I just hoped no one unfriendly stumbled upon me.

Before I could make my decision, my eyes grew heavy, and I was out.

Dreams were rarely fun for me. Sure, I had the occasional sexy dream, especially now that I had three more-than-worthy men to dream about, but usually, my dreams were filled with all the things I pushed down deep inside. This dream was nothing like the insecure guilt-ridden dreams I was used to having.

In this one, I was running through the forest. My body felt heavier than usual, and my feet moved with precision as if I knew the land like the back of my hand. Two others ran at my sides as we raced through the trees. There was panic in my chest and an overwhelming guilt weighing on my heart.

I didn't have time to think about the feeling because we came to a halt in the middle of the woods. My nostrils flared as I tried to pick up the scent of something. As my eyes scanned the surrounding area, I realized my companions were Firestar and Raiden. They sniffed the air as well, searching for something.

"Are you sure she went this way?" Raiden asked,

worry in his voice. His usual cheery face was pinched with emotion.

"I'm sure." The low growl that came from my voice surprised me, and I realized who exactly I was.

Jack.

Why the heck I was dreaming of being in his body was an unsettling thought. I had been thinking about him but not to the extent that I might dream of being him. Maybe I subconsciously wanted to make him pay for what happened? Or wanted to reassure myself that he felt bad about it? Whatever the reason, I couldn't think about it now because they were on the move again.

"There," I shouted, or rather Jack shouted, pointing a finger toward a familiar set of trees. We took off once more, shoving through the thick branches without care. My feet dodged and jumped over things I remembered tripping over not long ago. Suspicion filled me as I realized I might not just be dreaming.

When we broke through the tree line and came into sight of the river, I knew I wasn't dreaming. Or rather I was, and my mind had decided to body jump. I wasn't only dreaming of Jack. I was Jack, and he, along with Raiden and Firestar, were trying to find me.

"I smell blood." Firestar prowled forward, his eyes fierce as he searched the area. Anger flashed across his face as his fiery gaze landed on me. Or Jack. Whatever. "And that bitch of yours."

"Ex," I corrected. "She's very much an ex, and I never meant for any of this to happen."

"Of course, you didn't." Raiden clapped a hand on Jack's shoulder with a wry grin.

"Seriously," Jack growled, shaking Raiden's hand off his shoulder. "I only meant to show Gretchen that I was taken. I wouldn't be coming back to her, no matter what she did."

"Fat lot of good that did." Firestar swept a hand around the area where Gretchen and I had fought. My eyes zeroed in on the droplets of blood from the wound Gretchen had inflicted on me.

"Yes," Jack murmured with grief in his voice. "It does seem that my plan backfired. I'd never thought it would make Gretchen even more determined to get me back."

"Women are crazy." Raiden shrugged. "They never react the way you expect."

"Speaking of women, where is ours?" Firestar interrupted as he knelt by a rather large puddle of my blood. No wonder it hurt so much. I'd definitely have scars now.

"The lack of a body is a good sign, right?" Raiden raised a brow, a hopeful grin on his face. "That means she got away at least."

"I wouldn't be so certain of that." Jack shook his head, his hair whipping us in the face. "I know Gretchen. If she killed Maya, she wouldn't want evidence. She'd know we would come looking for her. She couldn't just leave Maya here."

"But she might not have killed her though," Raiden argued, stepping over to where Firestar stood. His eyes searched the ground, no doubt looking for any signs that I might still be alive.

I tried to scream, "I'm right here!" but my cries fell on deaf ears. Apparently, I was only a spectator in this experience.

The guys grew quiet for a moment, each of them lost in thought. Even though I was in Jack's head, I couldn't hear his thoughts. What's the point of being stuck in his head if his thoughts were closed off to me?

Raiden made a surprised sound, drawing Jack and Firestar's attention. He pointed a hand at the ice in the middle of the river. There was a body size hole in the water as well as some specks of blood from where I had skidded across the ice.

"Do you think …?" Raiden asked, his eyes wide with fear.

Firestar shook his head. "If Maya fell in, the likelihood that she made it …"

"… is dismal," Jack finished for him. The sadness in his voice pulsated through me. It was so intense that I was sure if I had been physical, it would have incapacitated me. Did Jack love me that much?

"We can't think like that." Raiden clenched his fists and shook his head rapidly. "We have to believe she made it. Maya is the strongest person I have ever met. She deals with us on a daily basis, right?"

Firestar visibly swallowed and inclined his head. "Right. She wouldn't give up so easily, and we can't either. Come on, let's follow downstream and see if she shows."

Instead of following after Firestar and Raiden, Jack held back, calling out toward Raiden. "Wait! What about your brothers?"

Raiden stopped to think that over. "Fujin and Raijin went around the other side," he explained. "Even still healing, they weren't about to let her go out on her own any more than we were. If we don't find her first, I'm sure they will."

Jack's lips pressed into a thin line, but he didn't argue. With a nod of his head, he followed after them, along the river current where I had gone. The prospect of seeing them made me fight against the dream. I wanted to be awake to see them when they found me.

Abruptly, I was thrust out of Jack and back into my body. But when I opened my eyes, I wasn't in the woods anymore. My little fire was gone, and the trees that had been a shoddy shelter were replaced by a stone cave. I tried to shoot to my feet, but the pain in my back caused me to cry out and collapse back onto the ground.

"I wouldn't do that if I were you," a voice cackled from somewhere in the cave.

"Who are you?" I asked, glaring into the darkness. "Why have you taken me?"

"I am a friend," was the mysterious answer I received, followed by, "and why else would I take you but to save you."

"I was fine on my own." I winced as I tried to sit up once more, not really helping my case.

"I see that," the voice cackled. I could tell by the feminine tone that it was a woman, an older woman from what I could tell. "But you would not have survived long enough for your men to arrive."

"You don't know that!" I argued, panic filling me. The guys were on their way to find me. How would they know that I wasn't there? They'd think I was dead.

"Oh, I do," the woman continued. "I know quite a lot of things about you, actually." She finally revealed herself, coming out of the shadows with a razor-sharp grin that made me cringe. "Or are you not Maya Rose of the Western Kingdom?"

"You really should stop moving around," the old woman, who introduced herself as Patrice. It was a fancy name for a lady living in a cave. I'd have expected something along the lines of Agda or Morma.

Hunched over and slightly limping, Patrice wasn't pretty by any means. Her hair was unkempt and skin too rough looking. I got a whiff of Patrice as she came closer to me, making my nose crinkle. Ick. Apparently, personal hygiene was not something of importance to her.

Before I could stop her, Patrice prodded at my back, and a shooting pain went through me. "Hey! What do you think you are doing?"

"Stop your whining," Patrice scoffed before she

started to dig around in the massive array of crap in her cave. I tried to get up again, but she shoved me down with an impressive amount of strength for an old hag.

"What are you going to do to me?" I asked, wincing as something cold touched my back. Before I knew it, I was screaming as pure agony poured through my back. If I thought it was on fire before, now it was like hot daggers were being shoved into my skin, biting into the bone beneath.

"It'll get better, just give it a minute."

Though the words were supposed to be reassuring, they didn't make the pain go away. Gritting my teeth until I thought they might break, I waited for the supposed pain to ebb. I wasn't sure how long it lasted, but just as I was about to pray for death, the pain ended abruptly.

"There you go, like new. Or sort of." Patrice shrugged and moved away from me.

I eased up, afraid the pain would come back, but happily, it stayed gone. I tried to touch the wounds because I was a glutton for punishment, but all I found was smooth skin. I dug under my top, surprised as I realized all evidence of my injury had disappeared.

Glancing up at Patrice who watched with a knowing smile, I asked, "What was in that stuff?"

"Nothing much." Patrice shrugged as she threw another bundle of sticks on the fire. She stirred a pot she had hanging over the fire, and a foul smell filled the cave ... well, fouler.

"Dare I ask what's in the pot? A curse or maybe poison to stop your enemies?" I climbed to my feet and stretched, happy to have the full range of my body back.

Patrice glowered at me. "My dinner."

My face dropped, and I ducked my head. "Sorry, didn't mean to offend." I tapped my hands against my legs, glancing around the place as I tried to figure out how I was getting out of there. "Not that I'm not grateful for your healing me and all, but I think I had better get going." I shuffled toward the door, but Patrice's voice stopped me.

"Don't you want to know your future?"

The age-old question, wasn't it? Definitely not something I'd have expected to come from Patrice, but then again, why else would she choose to live out in the woods if not because she had some hidden power?

After the way she healed my wounds in the blink of a painful eye, I was willing to buy into her words, especially with what I had been told about the gift of foresight the northern people were supposed to have.

"What about my future?" I slowly walked back toward her, my interest more than a little piqued.

"How about some dinner first? You must be hungry after all that fighting." Patrice slopped some of the foul-smelling contents of the pot into a bowl and offered it to me with a grin.

On its own accord, my nose scrunched up in disgust, but the prospect of learning my future made me force a smile on my lips. "Sure, I'd love to have dinner with you."

Patrice gestured for me to take a seat right where I had woken up, and with a reluctant sigh, I flopped back down on the fur-covered ground. Patrice handed me the bowl, no spoon of course, and as I stared down into it, bile rose. It looked to be a mixture of some kind of beef stew and rotten eggs. Cows didn't roam this area of Waesigar, so the likelihood that it was actually beef was pretty low.

"Eat, eat. It is good for the baby," Patrice urged me with a wave of her hand.

My eyes moved to her at the mention of my pregnancy. "How did you know I was pregnant?"

Patrice shrugged a shoulder and scooped herself

a bowl of slop. "How do I know you have three mates, all of whom have gained great powers by laying with you? Or that your cousin is hell-bent on taking the throne?" She paused for a moment before saying with a twinkle in her eyes, "I just know."

I watched her, my curiosity flaring the more she spoke. Sure, she might have heard about my guys through the grapevine, but the information about Ned? Only a few knew about his desire to take me out of the way so he could rule the Western Kingdom. That meant she was either a spy or psychic. Since she lacked the general qualities needed for a spy, I'd have to go with psychic.

"So ..." I drew out as she sat down beside me. "What can you tell me about my future?"

Ignoring my question, Patrice brought her bowl up to her mouth and began to slurp the contents. Taking as a hint, I let out a frustrated sigh and lifted my own bowl up. Nose scrunched up, I tried not to smell it as I took a hesitant gulp.

While the stew might have smelled horrid, the taste wasn't so bad, though the texture left a little to be desired. The slimy chunks were a bit hard to swallow.

Patrice glanced at me with an expectant look as

I swallowed thickly.

"It could use a bit of salt," was the best answer I could muster.

Seemingly satisfied with my words, Patrice went back to her meal. I set my bowl aside. While the stew wasn't the worst thing I'd ever eaten, I still couldn't stomach the rest without throwing it back up.

Clucking my tongue and rocking back on my hands, I asked, "So, why did you decide to live out here?" I scanned the cave that looked like it belonged on Extreme Hoarders Survival Style. I really didn't know how she found anything in this place.

"Didn't have much choice in the matter," Patrice informed me as she went back to the pot, scooping more into her bowl.

Seconds? Really?

Not voicing my inner disgust, I tried to keep the conversation going. Maybe if I showed interest in Patrice, she'd tell me what I wanted to know.

"What happened?"

Patrice sniffed. "The usual. Our people are known for having the foresight, some of us more than others. I happen to be in the small percentage of northerners who have far more control over their abilities than most."

"So, you can see whatever you want to see?" I cocked my head to the side, now truly interested in hearing about her.

Shaking her head, she scoffed. "If only it were that easy." Sitting back down next to me, Patrice didn't start eating her second helping right away, instead staring down at it like it deep in thought. "I see what the gods let me see. Sometimes I can direct it with strong intentions, but even then, I don't get the full picture."

"Can you see the past as well?"

"Pfft. Who wants to see that?" Patrice snorted and chugged her bowl. Belching loudly, she tossed the bowl on the ground before her. "What's done is done. Obsessing over it won't do any good."

"Why stay out here though? Your powers have to be highly sought after. You could even charge people to see their future. Humans do it all the time, except those people are usually faking, just stealing people's money. But you could have a nice house and not ..." I waved a hand to the mess around us. "… live in a cave."

"Bah!" Patrice cried. "I had that and more.

Don't you think I know how desired my abilities are, girl?" She spoke to me like I was soft in the head. "Dragons would come from all of Waesigar to beg a favor from me. Everyone and their mother wanted to know their future, no matter how bleak it was."

"Then what happened? Why live here?"

Patrice sighed and shook her head. "Gifts come with a price, and that price was privacy." Shuffling to her feet, she gathered up the bowls, setting them to the side. She grabbed a bottle filled with dark liquid and took a swig. I almost asked for one but thought better of it. More than likely it was alcohol, and I didn't want to hurt my child any more than it had been from the freezing cold water.

"Day in and day out, dragons would pour into my home, begging me to tell them their future. I couldn't even walk down the street without being attacked by some future seeker. It got exhausting."

"I could imagine."

While being able to see the future might seem like something totally cool and enterprising, I could see how it could get tiring. Who wanted to be constantly pestered by customers? It had to be the way celebrities in the human world felt when fans and paparazzi followed them around.

"Don't get me started on those whose futures

weren't exactly bright," Patrice growled, taking another gulp of the dark liquid. The sharp smell coming from her confirmed it was indeed some kind of alcohol. Dragon's Tears was clear so what kind of booze that was, I couldn't tell.

"They come to find out if their true love will ask them to be their mate, and no matter how much I tell them they don't want to know, they would beg and plead with me to tell them." Patrice sighed dramatically. "Then they end up doing something horrible because their mate was leaving them for their sister, or some other such nonsense."

"That's horrible." I shook my head sadly. "I'd hate to be a bearer of such bad news."

"Tell me about it." Patrice rolled her eyes. "So, I gave up the money and the fame to come out here. Sure, it gets lonely, but at least no one can blame me for their future."

"Hmmm." I mused. I could see how solitude could be a better option, though I knew I wouldn't have been able to handle it myself. I like my privacy as much as the next person, but I liked indoor plumbing and electricity. Not having a cell phone here was bad enough. I really needed to take a trip to Earth to check my messages. Also, I'd been dying for some video games.

"Anyway, my personal misery aside." Patrice finished the bottle off in a chug that would have made my friend Bianca proud. "Once I saw your predicament, I knew I had to make an exception. After all, it's not every day you meet someone as interesting at you."

I flushed at her words. "I'm not all that fascinating."

Patrice made a choking noise. "I'd have to disagree. You've been banished and then brought back and thrown at some of Waesigar's more eligible dragons. Then in an amusing twist of fate, you not only pick both the men your father offers you but add one of your own to the mix. Not that I can blame you." She gave me a mischievous grin followed by a wink. "If I were a few hundred years younger, I'd have done the exact same."

My face heated at her words. "I didn't exactly choose them all on purpose. They just sort of happened." Patrice gave me a disbelieving look. "Okay, okay. So, Firestar was an exception, but Jack and Raiden, you try picking just one of them." I crossed my arms over my chest with a scowl. "Not as easy as it looks."

"I'm not judging, dearie." Patrice laughed, making me glower all the more. "I just wonder how you handle all that delicious dragon flesh at once. It'll be even more entertaining when the others come."

That had me straightening up. "Others? What others?"

Patrice leered at me as she leaned forward as if to tell me a secret. "You know, the others."

"No, I don't know." I shook my head, refusing to acknowledge what she was implying. "I have my hands full enough with three guys. I don't have any room for more, now or ever."

"You say that now," - Patrice wagged a finger at me with a smirk - "but you will find your heart has more room in it than you realize."

I blew out a harsh breath. This old lady wasn't going to let up. She might be an all-powerful seer, but I couldn't accept it. Three was enough, more than enough. Sometimes even too much for me to handle. More than that would be ridiculous.

"So, that's all you see in my future?" I scoffed. "More men?"

"I didn't say that." Patrice shrugged a shoulder with a mysterious curve of her lips.

I shifted forward and put my hand on her arm. "Don't hold out on me now. You've brought me here for this very reason after all, haven't you?"

Patrice glanced at me with a menacing grin. "The men in your life will be the least of your worries when the world learns of your child and what she will become."

"She?" I inched forward. "It's going to be a girl."

"Of course!" she cried her face full of excitement. "Do you think a male would be able to handle all the powers she will inherit without becoming corrupt?" Patrice shook her head in disgust. "I think we've learned by now that the men of our world do not do well with too much power. Only she will be able to handle it all and join our world in the peace we long for."

"So, my daughter will be some all-powerful being?" My mouth dropped open, in awe of her predictions. I could hardly handle the powers I had, or rather the power to give others powers, let alone be the mother of someone with even greater powers.

Patrice seemed to sense my worry and said, "Do not worry, you will not be alone in this. Your mates will be there to help you, but to keep her truly safe, you will need all of them, even if your head is telling you otherwise."

She didn't say anything else after that, her eyes

focused on the fire in front of us. That was fine by me. I couldn't handle any more news. She had been right about knowing one's future. The things we learn may not be what we want to know, even if that something would redefine your whole existence.

19

I'd never seen myself as someone who would rule one day, even now that I was the technical heir to the throne.

Aeis had always been the one who was going to rule and, before that, my brother. But when he died in the last great dragon war, that burden fell on my sister. I never even thought I'd have a chance at it. Why my father thought I would even bother to try to usurp her was beyond me. Maybe someone was whispering little ideas in his ear, making him paranoid about his own family.

To be honest, going to the human world was one of the best things that had ever happened to me. I got away from dragon politics and found out there was more to the world than fighting and procreation. Like seeing who could eat a large pizza with everything the fastest, or even staying up for twenty-four hours to see who can get the highest score on the latest first-person shooter.

You know, the little stuff.

Humans knew how to enjoy themselves without making it all about bloodshed. No, I wasn't under any kind of delusions that they didn't have their fair share of killing and wars. I'd read some of their histories, and it made some of our own wars seem benign. Still, they knew what it took to keep their people happy, even if it was with silly things like the latest video game or a fifty percent off shoe sale. That was better than playing with their love lives so their parents could prosper.

God, I missed Ryan and Bianca. All the dragon politics was driving me mad, and if Patrice's visions were true, they weren't going to ease up anytime soon. They might even get worse when my daughter arrives. But I wouldn't do to her why my father did to me. No, sir!

My hand curled into a fist, and I pounded it against the ground. Patrice gave me a curious look but went back to staring at the fire without a word.

My daughter wouldn't be offered up like a

broodmare. Sure, I had found my mates that way, but I'd already found one before that. Who was to say I wouldn't have found Jack and Raiden on my own, without my father's interference? Nevertheless, because of him, I had more danger in my life than ever before, with a lack of power to deal with it.

Still, I got my wings because of it, something I'd wanted for longer than I could remember. And now we had a chance of joining the kingdoms together into a real peace, not this false one that my father pretends to desire.

Why was he allowing so many raids to happen? Did he know that Ned was after me? If my father really was the great leader he claimed to be, he wouldn't be letting these things happen right under his nose.

"He doesn't know." Patrice's voice interrupted my thoughts.

"Doesn't know what?" I asked, not believing for a moment that she had read my mind.

"I didn't. Read your mind that is." Patrice's lips turned up into a knowing grin, which made it hard to believe her. She waved a hand at my face. "Your thoughts are all over your face. You really should learn to control your emotions better."

Ignoring her dig, I asked again, "Who doesn't

know what?"

"Your father, of course. Lord Dannon, like all the lords, only sees what he wants to see. Some of them have long ago stopped seeing the big picture. That war will do nothing but beget more war and not give them what they truly desire."

"And what's that?"

She gave me a knowing smile but kept her mouth closed.

"Oh, come on," I complained, throwing my hands up in the air. "You've told me so much already. What is this one more thing?"

"Some things are better not known." Patrice started to say something else, but her eyes went from me to the opening of the cave. Shifting in place, she nodded in my direction. "They will be here soon. You should get ready. You have much ahead of you still to face."

"They?" My eyes darted to where she looked, seeing nothing but the barren trees outside the door. "Who are they?"

Patrice just smiled.

That's when I heard it, mixed voices and the rustling of feet. I jumped up, my hand going for my dagger before I realized I didn't have it. Cursing, I turned back to Patrice, only to see she was gone. In fact, the entire cave was different. All the piles of junk, the pot of disgusting stew, all gone. Only the fire remained.

"In here!" Raijin's voice became more distinguishable. A few seconds later, his long hair came into view of the cave's mouth, and I hurried forward.

"Raijin?" I frowned. "What are you doing here?"

Raijin rushed into the cave, his hands going to my arms as he looked me over. When I had passed his assessment, he sighed. "Looking for you, of course. You've been missing for hours. Your guys are going out of their minds with worry."

"Well, sorry to disappoint, but I'm fine." I smiled up at the twin just as his other half came barreling into the cave. "Fujin!"

"Maya!" Fujin shoved his brother out of the way and spent his own time assessing me. "You're alive and well."

"Yes, I am," I answered, chuckling at their concern.

Fujin released me suddenly, making me stumble.

"Then why the hell are you still out here? Do you have any idea how crazed you have made us all?"

"All?" I cocked a brow at the two of them who blanched at my question.

"You know," Fujin cleared his throat and waved a hand. "The whole of everyone. Even Lord Fafnir has called a search for you."

Since I was feeling charitable, I let the subject drop. "Well, as you can see, I'm fine. At least, as fine as I can be after having been attacked and then left for dead. So, if you could kindly lead the way, I'd like a hot bath and a large dessert. Something preferably in the chocolate department."

Fujin and Raijin smiled at me and offered me their arms as they led me from the cave. As we stepped out of it, a voice tickled my brain that had me pause.

"To gain is to lose. Your biggest fight is yet to come." Patrice's voice rippled through my mind.

How she was able to project into my head made me wonder if she had actually been able to read my mind. Or had she been a figment of my imagination all along? The guys hadn't seen her, after all.

"Maya?" Fujin asked, jarring me from my thoughts. "Are you, all right?"

"Yeah, yes." I quickly changed my answer,

shaking my head. "Still a little shaken up by the whole thing."

Raijin patted my hand. "I'd imagine. When Firestar and the others saw your blood by the river, they were beside themselves with worry. But I knew you could take care of yourself."

"You did, did you?" I smiled up at him.

"Of course!" Raijin chuckled, throwing an arm around my shoulders. "Anyone who could put up with those three has to have a hell of a survival instinct."

"I don't know about that," I grumbled, enjoying the twin's arm around me a bit more than I wanted to admit.

Patrice's words came back to me as the twins helped me through the woods. More men. Could the twins possible be those she had talked about? The very idea was ridiculous. They had just gone to war with their mother over the very fact. For me to take them into my bed after all that would be, as I said, ridiculous.

Right?

Still, something nagged at me as we walked along. Patrice had said I would gain others, but also, I'd lose something in return. I didn't have much to my name to lose. My daughter and my men were all that had any value to me. Even the kingdom was negotiable.

My mind was so distracted that I didn't see the tree limb until after my foot snagged on it. I tumbled to the ground, my hands burning as they skidded against the rocks and branches beneath me. I gasped and came to my knees, Fujin and Raijin quick to kneel by my side.

"Here, let me see." Raijin took my hand in his hand and picked away the debris. Beneath were angry red scratches that were just this side of bleeding. "You need to be more careful. One sharp stick and you could have been lost something precious."

I frowned at his chastising tone. "I didn't trip on purpose. I have a lot on my mind."

"I can imagine." Fujin scoffed. "We all have had more than our fair share of trouble lately. It makes one crave the more peaceful times."

"Did those ever exist?" Raijin asked with dry humor.

I chuckled and rose to my feet. "They'll happen again. We just have to get through all of our parents' hell-bent desire on keeping us in the old ways and stay alive while doing it."

"Piece of cake," Fujin said, and Raijin followed, "Piece of crumb cake."

"You guys are so thinking the wrong way." I laughed as we started our journey once more. "The only kind of cake this will turn into is the kind that bleeds."

"As all wars do," Fujin added.

Raijin snorted. "Don't I know it."

20

By the time the twins got me back to the village, the sun had started to set. I didn't even get a foot into the village before I was surrounded on all sides by my guys and worried villagers.

"Are you okay?" Raiden asked, grabbing my shoulders like his brothers had before him.

"I'm all right." I let him fret over me for a moment before I pushed his hands away. Unfortunately, right after him came Firestar.

"You're not fine. There was blood, we saw it. Show me your wound," Firestar growled, the demanding, protective tone in his voice hitting all the right places in me.

I held my hands up and spun around in a circle. "Look all you want. You will find nothing. Though," I purred, trailing my fingers up and down Firestar's chest, "I'd be willing to undergo an extensive strip search."

Firestar grabbed my finger, baring his teeth at me. "That's not funny. You could have died." He pressed his forehead against mine, his eyes staring intently into mine.

Seeing the worry there, I wrapped my arms around his waist and leaned into him. "I'm sorry. You're right. It wasn't funny, but I assure you, I'm fine."

"Still," Jack stepped in, placing a hand on my shoulder. "You should let Trina check you out. Make sure the baby is all right."

I met Jack's concerned gaze and realized that this hurt him even more than the others. I guess I couldn't blame him. He was what that caused me to run off on my own. The guilt I had felt inside of him while I was dreaming had to be roaring. It would be even more so when he found out who exactly was responsible for my disappearance.

Nodding, I stepped out of Firestar's embrace. "Yes, of course. That's a good idea."

Surrounded by my men, who barely let me more than a foot away from them as we marched toward Lord Fafnir's home, with the uncomfortable multitude eyes on me and almost tripping over my own feet, I'd had enough.

Coming to a halt, I was almost run over by Firestar at my back. Hands up, I spun on the guys who all had matching confused looks. "I love you guys, but I need some space."

The guys exchanged a look, and then Firestar asked, "What do you mean ... space?"

I waved my hands around to indicate my personal bubble. "I mean physical space." When they still looked at me as if I were speaking another language, I added, "Meaning, I love you, and I understand how worried you were, but I can't walk on my own with you all so close to me."

Like a light bulb had gone off, I was met with an equal amount of embarrassment on each of their faces. They all took a step back, and it was like I could breathe again.

"Thanks," I muttered and turned back toward the house, my feet moving a bit faster than before. The guys were quiet as we entered the building and I worried I might have hurt their feelings. Hoping to break the tension, I made small talk. I hated small talk.

"So, who won?" I crossed my arms over my chest, scuffing my feet on the ground as we walked.

"Won?" Raiden asked.

"You know, the hunt." I glanced at him with a raised brow. "I kind of missed, well, all of it, but surely you guys heard something?"

They exchanged a look over my head before Jack frowned at me. "We don't know. We spent most of the day looking for you."

"Looking for me?" I scoffed, suddenly angry with them. "Even if you found the blood trail, it was Raiden's brothers who actually found me. What, did you get lost after following the very straight river?"

"Hey," Firestar grabbed my arm, stopping me in my tracks. "We were doing the best we could, searching for someone who didn't want to be found. If you had stayed close to us like we wanted, none of this would have happened."

I shook Firestar's arm off and glared at Jack. "And if someone hadn't been getting handsy to make his ex mad, I wouldn't have taken off, and she wouldn't have gotten all handsy on me."

"What?" Jack asked, his voice rising more than

I'd ever heard before. "What do you mean, she got handsy? She hurt you? Where? Show me."

Jack pulled at my clothes, and I slapped his hands away with a growl. "Back off. I'm not about to strip down here in the hallway, and besides, it's gone now. Nothing to see."

"Gone? How?" Raiden asked as he tried to usher us toward our rooms, so we didn't draw any more attention to ourselves.

I kept my mouth shut until we were safe behind my bedroom door. Getting out from between the guys, I went over to my bag and dug through it for something comfortable. Pulling my shirt over my head, I was met with a mixture of gasps and growls.

"What happened?" Jack rumbled, his hand touching my back where I knew there was nothing to see. "There's blood but no wound. How can this be?"

I shrugged. "While you guys were chasing your tails, I got rescued by this old woman. She's a seer, I think." I frowned and shook my head, still not a hundred percent sure of what had happened.

"A seer?" Jack asked, his brows rising. "I haven't heard of anyone being an actual seer in a long time, not since the great Seer, Patrice, left us."

"That would be her, all right." I sighed and

made for the bathroom. My skin itched, and my hair felt like it had a mountain of dirt in it. Turning on the water to the shower, I shimmied out of my pants.

Three sets of eyes burned into my back. I might have blushed at all the attention, but the day had been too long. I wanted to just scrub it away and forget it ever happened.

"So," Raiden started, not even trying to hide how his eyes swept over my bare skin, "this seer, Patrice. She healed you, I'm assuming?"

"Yeah." I stepped into the shower and raised my voice as I spoke. "She has some killer healing powers, they burn like a bitch by the way but really work. Just don't try her cooking," I quickly added, wagging a finger out the shower door.

"How bad were you hurt?" Firestar asked, his voice muffled because my head was under the faucet.

Sighing, I quickly scrubbed my hair and rinsed before ducking out of the water. I'd have to do a better job later when there weren't so many questions to be answered. Jack handed me a towel which I gladly took.

Taking my sweet time drying off, I bathed in

their admiring looks. After the day I had, a girl needed all the good feelings she could get. The guys waited patiently - far longer than I would have - for me to answer.

I wrapped the towel around me and sat on the edge of the tub. Leveling my eyes on their collective stares, I sighed and settled my gaze on Jack. "Your ex packs quite a punch, or rather claw. I might have died had it not been for the seer."

I told them what happened with Gretchen. All the gory details, even my plunge into my potential ice death. The guys handled it better than I expected. There were only a few roaring outbursts, most of them from Jack, who I thought might actually have a heart attack, if he didn't rip Gretchen's throat out first.

"I'm going to kill her," Jack snarled, heading for the bedroom door. Jumping up from the bathtub, we hurried after him. Before Jack could leave, Firestar cut him off, blocking his path. "Get out of my way."

"You need to think about this," Firestar argued, not budging an inch. "We need these people to help us and killing one of them won't endear us to anyone."

"But she hurt Maya." Jack glanced my way, his teeth bared. "She could have killed our child. Don't you want her to pay?"

"Of course, I do." Firestar shook his head. "But I also know that going after her in a blind rage is not the way."

I snorted, causing the two to look my way. "What?" I shrugged and gave Firestar a wry grin. "You have to admit, you giving advice on keeping one's head is pretty funny."

Firestar tried to argue, but Raiden, who had been watching from the side, interrupted. "So, this seer healed you and at no point did you think to ask about your future?"

I opened my mouth, but no words came out. I had asked, but I wasn't so sure the guys would like what she said. No, I knew for sure that they wouldn't like it. Well, maybe the part about our daughter - not the all-powerful part though - but not the adding to the list of people in my bed or my heart.

Jack stopped trying to get past Firestar and turned to me. "Maya? What did she say?"

"Not much." Chewing on my thumb, I stared down at the ground. I didn't want to lie, but I didn't want to hurt them either.

"Maya," Jack said my name with a bit more warning in it this time. Instead of trying to get through Firestar, Jack's anger had turned on to me. "What did she tell you?"

Glancing up from the floor to meet their expectant eyes, I dropped my arms and let out an over exaggerated breath. "Ugh. We're going to have a girl, and she's going to be a super dragon. Not like powerful vagina powers to gift others with - thank god for small favors." I chuckled briefly but didn't get the expected laughs in return. "But anyways, she's going to be like this big bad that'll combine the whole of Waesigar."

Raiden made a whooping noise, his face lighting up at the news. "A daughter, yes!"

Jack gave him a pointed look before turning back to me. "That's it?" Jack stepped closer to me.

His expression was unreadable, something I didn't like. I scurried backward, clutching my towel to me, though really what was the point? My back hit the wall as Jack caged me in with his arms.

"Maya," he growled, the heat of him sinking into my skin, making my thighs press together to stave off the sudden bout of need.

"I-I ..." I licked my lips and swallowed deeply. This back and forth with my hormones was really giving me some major whiplash. One minute I was madder than a teenage girl ditched at prom, and then the next I was that same teenage girl ready to hump in the back of her boyfriend's daddy's Cadillac. It was really confusing.

"You what, Maya," he murmured, his mouth closing in on mine.

My eyes darted from Jack to Raiden and Firestar who didn't seem the least concerned by our ice man's out of character actions. Firestar simply crossed his arms over his chest and raised a brow. And Raiden! Raiden, the cheeky bastard, grinned like the idiot that he sometimes seemed to be.

"Answer him, Maya," Firestar smirked, and I glared at him.

Not able to handle all the testosterone in the room anymore, I put my hands up between Jack and me, easing him away from me. "Look, you won't like it. I don't really know what it means, anyway."

"Just tell us," Jack insisted, only backing off enough to let me breathe.

I ran a hand through my still-wet hair and tugged the towel a bit closer. "She didn't give me much. Something about how to gain is to lose, and I have more room in heart than I think." I shrugged and raised a brow, looking at them to see if they had come to the same conclusion as me.

Jack moved further away from me, his gaze locking with Raiden and Firestar. "Any ideas what that means?"

Raiden tucked his hands into his pockets and smacked his lips. "Nope. I've never been good at riddles."

"Me either." Firestar sighed and then looked at me. "Are you sure that's all she said?"

"Yep," I popped the end of the word, hoping none of them caught that I had left out some important parts. While that had been what Patrice had said, I still didn't want to cause more issues than we already had. Emotions were high enough. Revealing more might make them go ballistic. Then Gretchen wouldn't be the only one who would need to be watching their backs.

"Very well." Jack nodded and offered me his hand. I slid mine into his cool one and let myself give into the comfort of his touch. "Let's get you checked out, shall we?"

"What about Gretchen? I thought you were going to kill her?" I cocked my head to the side.

Jack's lip curled up at the edges. "She can wait. Our daughter cannot. We have to make sure everything's ticking right if she's going to be the glue that brings our kingdoms together, right?"

I pressed my lips together tightly. "Right."

21

"Take a deep breath in, and out," Trina advised as she passed her glowing hands over me. They settled on my stomach, and that familiar but still strange tingling feeling filled me.

My eyes met my anxious mates. I didn't need to be a mind reader to know we were all worried about Trina's diagnosis. I'd been beaten by Gretchen and the rocks beneath the ice, not to forget the freezing water I'd been submerged in. It'd be a miracle if our child was still in one piece.

I didn't know how I felt about that. I'd complained and blamed my pregnancy for all my current problems, most of that hormone related. But for some reason, knowing that it will be a girl made my pregnancy seem all the more real, like she wasn't just some bundle of cells inside of me hell bent on making me miserable.

Plus, she was going to be an all-powerful ruler someday. The one to join all of Waesigar together. How could I want anything but for her to be good and well? Though, that part didn't make my nervousness about being a mother any better.

Being a parent was hard enough. Being the parent of the savior of the dragons? Pfft. I had a feeling I would need all the help I could get and maybe a special stash of Dragon's Tears. That said, at least I wouldn't have to do it alone. My lips curved into a smile and my heart filled with appreciation for the men around me.

Yes, we had our differences, plenty of clashing personalities and butting of heads, not to forget the drama that is Gretchen. All that aside, I knew with complete certainty that they would be there for me through all of this. I wouldn't have to worry about being a single mother or even part of a pair. Four parents had to be better than two, right?

"The baby is fine," Trina announced with a small smile on her face. The tension in the room lifted as we all let out a much-needed breath. The guys crowded around me, each showing me their affection in their own way. I hopped off the table, thinking I was done, but Trina stopped me, her face no longer smiling.

"The baby is fine, but I still want to see you over the next couple of weeks to be sure nothing comes up." I nodded my head, not surprised she'd want to check up on me. Then she gave me her no-nonsense doctor face, and I knew I was in trouble. "I know you probably won't listen to me, but I'm going to say it, anyway. You are pregnant and have a target on your back. That means you can't go gallivanting off on your own whenever you get pissed off, which will be often, I have no doubt."

Firestar grunted in agreement, and Raiden chuckled. I shot them a glare which softened when Jack placed his hand on my shoulder.

I glanced up at him and sighed. "I know, I was reckless." Firestar snorted at that, making me shoot him a warning look. "I'll be more careful in the future." I gave a wry grin. "And believe me when I say I will not be going off on my own again." Well, anytime soon, but I was going to leave that unsaid.

"Good to hear." Trina nodded at me before turning her attention to the guys. "You need to take care of her. She's going to need you more now than ever. Being pregnant is hard enough without having to look over your shoulder. Focus on making things easier for Maya, the less stress, the better."

"Don't worry, Trina. We got this." Raiden clapped his hand on my shoulder a bit hard, and I winced. He quickly lifted his hand with a grimace. "Sorry."

Jack let out a huff and shook his head. "As Raiden so elegantly put it, we will do everything in our powers to make sure that Maya and our ... child," he caught himself before calling it our daughter. No one but us knew I had seen the seer, and it was probably best we kept it that way.

"I'm sure you will." Trina inclined her head to me before backing off from the table.

Firestar filled the spot Trina had left, his hand laying on my thigh. Even through my pants, I could feel the heat of him, warming my insides. I shifted on the table uncomfortably. I rarely had all three of them surrounding me like this. It excited me more than I expected.

I felt more than saw the guys tense around me. They each inhaled deeply, letting it out with a growl that rumbled through me. I prepared to have my final fantasy fulfilled when I let out a growl of my own ... except mine came from my stomach.

The sexual heat in the room was decimated as

the three of them broke out into laughter. Face flushing, I glared down at my stomach. Traitor.

Firestar offered me a hand, smirking. "Let's get you fed and then we can work on helping you relax." There was so much heat in his voice that my mouth went dry just hearing it. I didn't know what he had in mind, but I knew I would enjoy it … immensely.

We headed for the dining hall in companionable silence, the guys never once not touching me. It was funny how on the way to the house I had been feeling so trapped by their closeness. Now though, it seemed like I couldn't get close enough.

By the time we reached the dining room, my legs felt like they might fall out from under me, shaken loose by the need pulsating between my thighs. When the doors opened, and all eyes landed on us, my face heated. No doubt they could smell my desire, and I fought to push it down.

The guys were stiffening beside me for a different reason altogether. Gretchen sat at a table near us. The look on her face, a mixture of disbelief and horror, caused a wicked sort of grin to cover my lips.

Thought you got me, didn't you? Guess again.

Before any of us could react to Gretchen, Lord Fafnir and his son appeared before us.

"Ah, nephew." He smiled at Jack, but it was forced, making me think he could see the rage burning beneath the surface of his nephew's face. "I'm so glad to see that you and your mate are well." Lord Fafnir turned to me and took my hands in his, patting them with an apologetic grimace. "We were beside ourselves when we heard you had disappeared. We are overjoyed to find out you had been found and without a scratch on you."

"Thank you," I muttered, eyeing Jack out of the corner of my eye. We all knew I hadn't exactly come out unscathed, but how could I explain that to them and not have everything else come to the fore? That wasn't a conversation I wanted to have.

Jack finally broke his silence with a menacing growl. "I will not stand to see her here any longer, uncle."

"Now, Jack." Lord Fafnir frowned. "She has done nothing wrong. In some cases, others would still find you in the wrong for casting her aside so easily to take a foreigner into your bed."

"And whose fault is that?" Jack snapped, the first display of disrespect I'd ever seen from him toward Lord Fafnir. "None of this would have happened had I not done as you bid. While I have gained from the matter, no one can blame her for being upset at being tossed aside without any explanation from the leader who so dearly cared for her."

Hearing Jack talk about Gretchen that way didn't upset me. I understood. If I'd been in her position, I'd probably have gone a bit crazy as well. To have the man I loved leave me for no other reason than duty would have been devastating. Though, I'd have had the good sense to not attack said new mate or at least make sure she was actually dead when I went after her.

"What did you want me to do, Jack?" Lord Fafnir sighed. "Nothing I could have done or said would have appeased her."

"Well, you can do something now," Jack snarled before pushing past Lord Fafnir and striding toward where Gretchen sat. "Gretchen, you attacked my mate unprovoked and left her for dead. Do you deny it?"

Gretchen's eyes widened, and she scrambled to her feet as the gasps around us made her flush. "Jack, can we talk about this somewhere else? More private?" Her gaze darted around to the waiting dragons, all forgetting their meal to witness the drama unfolding.

"No, we will do this here, where all can hear your lies." Jack's voice was hard and cold as the ice he used. It even made me wince.

All my sympathy for her went out the window though when she placed her hand on Jack's chest as if she had the right to touch him. "Please, Jack, you have to understand how I feel."

"No," Jack snapped, shaking her hand off. "I don't. The only concern I have is for my mate and the safety of her and my unborn child, which you threatened. Now, tell me why I shouldn't kill you right here."

Gretchen's mouth dropped opened, and her gaze turned to me briefly before locking back onto Jack. "You have to believe me, I didn't know. If I'd known she was pregnant, I would have ..."

"You would have what? Made sure to dig your claws into her stomach rather than her back?" The accusation caused the collected audience in the room to gasp.

Shaking her head, Gretchen tried to cling to Jack's chest. "No, no. I didn't mean it. I was just so angry, and then there she was looking so smug at having what I didn't. I just lost it. I tried to save her, though. Did she tell you? When she fell on the ice, I tried to get her, but it was cracking too fast. Tell him!" Gretchen's eyes were wild as she pleaded for me to collaborate her story.

I remembered Gretchen coming onto the ice, but it wasn't to save me. If anything, it was to shove me further into it, to make sure I never got in the way of her and Jack again.

Jack's eyes went to me for a half a second. I shook my head, my eyes going to the floor. I didn't like this. He should have done this in private, not before everyone. How humiliating.

"He has to do this in public," Raiden whispered into my ear, holding me close to him. "Casting someone out from their nation requires a large audience, to make sure she never tries to come for him or his again."

"It's still not right," I muttered, leaning into his embrace.

"It has to be done," Lord Fafnir murmured with a reluctant sigh.

"I cast you out," Jack announced, his pale gaze firmly on hers before moving to those watching. "Let all here bear witness that I, Jack, nephew to the great Lord Fafnir, deny all existence of Gretchen of clan Norse. No longer will she walk in my sight or come near those I care for." His eyes then landed back on Gretchen who visibly wilted beneath his penetrating stare. "You are dead to me."

"No, no." She shook her head, her eyes welling up with tears. "You can't do this. What about all that we had? All that we were? You can't just forget about me. I won't allow it."

Her words fell on deaf ears when Jack turned his face from her as if she didn't exist. Even when her hands grabbed at him as he moved away, he didn't react to her beyond merely shaking her off. She really was dead to him.

As Gretchen collapsed to the ground in the middle of the dining hall, wailing like a banshee, a part of me felt bad for her. I know that I shouldn't have. She had tried to kill me, tried to take what was mine, but no one should have that done to them. A fate worse than death, it was.

Eventually, Gretchen's brothers came to her side, helping her to her feet as they tried to usher her from the room. The rest of the hall had long since gone back to their meals, pretending the crying woman didn't exist. Unfortunately, Gretchen hadn't learned her lesson. Before her brothers could escort her from the dining hall, she ripped away from their grasps and stalked toward us.

"The dagger," she gasped out as her brothers

caught her, pulling her away from us. "Please, just let me have the dagger. Just this one thing. Please!"

My hand instinctively went to the dagger sheath I had strapped on, though the dagger no longer sat in it. I'd have given it to her if I had it, but it was missing still. Her eyes went to where my hand touched, and her face fell.

"I'm sorry." I shook my head. "I don't have it. It was lost in the woods."

Nodding her head in acceptance, Gretchen allowed her brothers to take her away, leaving the hall to go back to their meals.

Jack stood next to his cousin, murmuring too low for me to hear. I tried to meet his gaze, but he wouldn't look at me. Frowning, I turned to Firestar. "Find it, will you? The dagger."

"Why?" Firestar shook his head. "You shouldn't care a lick about that woman. She tried to kill you. If anything, you should want the dagger for yourself, not to give to her."

Pain welled in my chest, and I clutched my hand to my heart. "You're a man. You don't understand. To love someone and not have them love you back is one thing, but for them to completely refuse your existence after having been loved by them ... it's pure torture. She will never find peace from this." I shook my head in sadness. "The least I can do is give her something to hold onto."

"You'll just make it worse for her." Raiden squeezed me to him. "You should want her to forget about him and you, not give her something to remember you by, to hate you for."

"Maybe I deserve it," I muttered, my own eyes filling with tears. "It's my fault she's like this. I took Jack from her, after all."

"No, it's not." Jack stepped in front of me, his hand tilting my face up. "That woman brought it on herself. You are too tender-hearted for your own good, and it will get you killed. Now, forget about her as I have."

I chewed on my lip and nodded slightly. I couldn't, though, no matter how much he told me to. I couldn't just forget about someone whose life I had ruined because, although she had made bad decisions, it was ultimately my fault.

They ushered me to a table and put food on my plate. I wasn't hungry any longer. I pushed my food around and pretended to eat, but my mind was on the devastation I had just witnessed.

Firestar sat at my side and seemed to notice my lack of appetite. He placed his hand on mine, applying pressure until I looked at him. With a knowing look in his eyes, he said, "If it eases your pain, I will find the dagger and deliver it to her."

"Really?" I asked, my eyes lighting up. "You'd do that for me?"

"Of course, I'd do that and more." Firestar lifted my hand to his mouth pressing his lips to it before pointing his fork at my plate. "Now, do something for me and eat."

Picking up my own fork, I smiled. "Gladly."

After dinner, I was ready to fall asleep where I stood. The guys seemed to be lost in their own thoughts and thankfully weren't in the mood to talk.

I'd had about as much thinking as I could handle for one day. Any more and my brain might implode.

Stopping before our bedroom doors, I started to go to mine, but stopped and turned to Jack. I couldn't leave things like they were.

"Do you want me to stay with you tonight?" I asked, wrapping my arms around myself. I half-wished he'd say no, but the other half wanted to be sure he was okay.

Jack shook his head, his hair swaying in front of him. "No, I think tonight, I'd like to be alone."

I nodded. "I understand, but if you need anything ..."

"I know." Jack stepped toward me and cupped my face in his hands. His lips brushed mine softly, and before I opened my eyes, he had already closed the door of his bedroom.

Sighing in dejection, I wrapped my arms around myself. "Anyone else feel like today just kind of sucked?"

Raiden gave a dry chuckle and slipped his arms around me. "Don't worry, it'll get better. Just give him time. And you ..." He ran his hands up and down my arms in a comforting gesture. "… need to get some sleep. Our daughter has had a trying day."

"The mother has had a trying day," Firestar corrected Raiden as from his spot against the wall. "One that we should end as soon as possible. How is Maya even standing right now?" He shook his head in disbelief.

A tired chuckle tumbled out of me, and I shifted out of Raiden's arms to punch Firestar in the arm. "I'm tougher than you give me credit for, you know."

"Ain't that right." Raiden snorted. "To deal with Mr. Hothead and the Ice King, I'm surprised you don't want to stab yourself."

"Hey! You're no prize either, Mister Never Can Be Serious," Firestar growled. "You'd laugh at your own mother's funeral." Silence fell over the hallway at Firestar's comment. His face dropped as he realized what exactly he had just said. "Raiden, man. I didn't mean it like that."

"No, don't worry about it." Raiden waved him off, a wry grin on his lips. "My mother's a bitch, but I still love her. Guess we all have our own hang-ups."

"And rightfully so." I hugged him closer to myself. "Now, if you two don't mind, I'm going to go bury myself in my bed. If I don't come out by noon, don't send in a search party."

Raiden chuckled and pressed his mouth to mine before going to his respective room.

Firestar pushed off the wall and took my hands in his. "I meant what I said. I'll find that dagger for you. At least one of us should have some peace of mind."

"Thank you." Swallowing thickly, I pressed my face into his chest inhaling deeply. Cinnamon and firewood, the smell of home. If I could bottle up my guys' scents, I would be a billionaire in the human world.

"Now, go get some sleep. We'll see you in the morning." Firestar ushered me toward my door, smacking me on the butt as he did.

I shot him a playful glare but broke down in giggles as I stepped into my room. Glancing around I sighed. Alone at last.

I went about my usual bedtime routine before slipping under the covers. Burrowing down into the plush mattress, for the first time in a while I was truly happy. Everything with my mates was good, not perfect, but good. We were getting men to rescue Raiden's father, and we had a daughter. Besides, Ned's head on a platter, nothing could make me happier.

THANK YOU FOR READING!

Curious about what happens to Maya, Raiden, Jack, and Firestar next?

Find out in Pounding Earth!

AUTHOR'S NOTE

Dear reader, if you REALLY want to read the next Starcrossed Dragons novel- I've got a bit of bad news for you. Unfortunately, **Amazon will not tell you when the next comes out.**

You'll probably never know about my next books, and you'll be left wondering what happened to Maya and the gang. That's rather terrible.

There is good news though! There are three ways you can find out when the next book is published:

1) You join our mailing list by clicking here.

2) You can also follow Erin on her Facebook Page. We always announce new books in those places as well as interact with fans.

3) You follow us on Amazon. You can do this by going to the store page (or clicking this link) and clicking on the Follow button that is under the author picture on the left side.

If you follow me, Amazon will send you an email when I publish a book. You'll just have to make sure you check the emails they send.

Doing any of these, or all three for best results, will ensure you find out about my next book when it is published.

If you don't, Amazon will never tell you about my next release. Please take a few seconds to do one of these so that you'll be able to join Maya and the gang on their next adventure.